Write

on the

Coast

An anthology of short stories, poetry and flash fiction

By

Westcliff-on-Sea Women's Institute
(WoSWI) Writing Group

Edited by Kim Kimber
(www.kimkimber.co.uk)

With thanks to
James Fanthorpe (@JamesLFanthorpe)
for the cover design and
Simon Woodward (www.srwoodward.co.uk)
for help with the publishing process.

Proceeds from this anthology are being divided between
Southend Hospital Brachytherapy Suite Appeal
(Registered Charity No. 1057266) and
Westcliff-on-Sea Women's Institute (WoSWI)
(Registered Charity No. XT 36711)

For all members of the
Women's Institute

Contents

Foreword

By Kim Kimber

I had no idea what to expect one year ago when several members from Westcliff-on-Sea Women's Institute (WoSWI) squeezed into my kitchen for the inaugural meeting of the newly formed writing group, or even if we would make it beyond that first night.

Fuelled by tea and cookies, we set out to discover what would happen when a group of women of varying ages and with different life experiences, put pen to paper. The assembled ladies ranged from enthusiastic beginners and those who had dabbled with writing in the past, to those of us who write professionally but not necessarily in the genre to which we aspire; closet novelists, secret poets and shy storytellers, each and every one.

The work in this book all stems from exercises started in the group, developed at home and brought to the next meeting to share and discuss with the aim of improving our writing. Each member of the group has their own ideas and individual writing style but we all have one thing in common; a love of the written word.

Along the way, some members have left, others have joined, most have stayed the course. From the outset, I was impressed by the wealth of talent in the group and publishing an anthology seemed like a good way to showcase members' work whilst raising money for an excellent cause. *Write on the Coast* is the result; a collection of short stories, poems, flash fiction and observations on life.

On behalf of myself and the members of WoSWI Writing Group, we hope that you will enjoy reading our anthology as much as we did writing it.

Jerusalem

By Lynda Brown

A monologue set in the hall of the Women's Institute.

The latecomer: "Am I too late or can you squeeze another one in? Perhaps if the large lady on your right - sorry, don't know your name love - could move over, you could all shunt your chairs one inch to the right. That's it. Oh, have you hurt yourself? I shouldn't wonder if she sat on the chair with the leg on your foot! I should have counted one, two, three and you could have all moved in unison. Sorry to be such a pain. And now we've all to stand again for *Jerusalem!* Would you mind turning the words a fraction in my direction? My eyes aren't what they used to be and my memory is even worse!"

> *And did those feet in ancient time,*
> *Walk upon England's mountains green?*
> "Has anyone seen Joyce?"
> *And was the holy Lamb of God,*
> "She said she was coming."
> *On England's pleasant pastures seen?*
> "She specially wants to hear our speaker tonight."
> *And did the Countenance Divine*
> "Can't say it's something I'm interested in."
> *Shine forth upon our clouded hills?*

3

"I'd rather go to bed with a hot chocolate and a good book."

And was Jerusalem builded here,

"But you have to keep up with the times Joyce says."

Among these dark Satanic Mills?

"They're all at it up North apparently, though my sister's not noticed. You alright Sandra?"

Bring me my bow of burning gold!

"Have you got over that fella yet?"

Bring me my arrows of desire!

"He was a nasty piece of work and she was a fool to go off with him."

Bring me my spear! O clouds, unfold!

"She'll regret it. She's lost all of us."

Bring me my chariot of fire!

"Can't show her face here again I should say."

I will not cease from mental fight,

"You lost weight Sheila?"

Nor shall my sword sleep in my hand,

"Or have you done your make-up differently?"

Till we have built Jerusalem

"It's taken 10 years off you."

In England's green and pleasant land.

"How are your bunions Gladys? Are we all ready for a drink now?"

Southend in the Rain

By Lois Maulkin

We were headed to the beach, which is often at its best, and certainly at its most spacious, in inclement weather. Raincoats on, and a flask of sustaining coffee in my bag, off we went into the grey dampness of a June afternoon in Southend, where vicious looking green leaves stood out sharply against a soft focus sky.

We passed a house with its front door standing open, showing a carpeted hallway containing a bamboo shelf full of someone's prized collection of tall, spotlessly clean, china figurines. Their precise positioning was guarded stiffly by an upright vacuum cleaner, on sentry duty to one side and apparently ready to suck up any joy or spontaneity that might dare to stumble in across the threshold. I had a moment of wondering if I was doing the right thing, or if I'd be better off turning back for home, opening the biscuit barrel and sitting everyone down in front of *Mulan*. However, scooters skidding damply over the dark pavements, on we headed.

Queen Victoria, parked regally in her accustomed place on the clifftop, her enormous workman's hand with its giant white saveloy finger extended, looked out glumly across the estuary. In the drizzle, her massive digit appeared to be a pistol she was pointing, ready to repel the men of Kent, should they make an attempt on Royal Terrace.

Patchwork-sided container ships ironed up and down the wrinkled water, looming heavily out of grey mist, under grey sky, across grey brine. Looking out across the waves was like looking at television in the old days, 27 shades of fuzzy grey. Raindrops polka dotted the surface of the sea, and pattered on my umbrella, and little waves crested with soft scum soothed out 'hush, hush, hush' as they met the sand.

I sipped my coffee. Clusters of seaweed bobbed perkily onto shore like embellished swimming caps from the '50s, re-coloured in modish black. Their shiny rubberiness vanished as soon as they reached the beach, and they lay there, having lost all sense of fun, as unlovely now as wet wigs in a dirty gutter. Beneath the heaps of exhausted flotsam, the sand was striped with shingle, like the lines of sunken sultanas in a less than totally successful light fruit cake, and as I mused on this thought, my tummy rumbled, and I realised the small puddle I'd accidentally sat down in had clambered stealthily halfway up my back. I made the decision to go home.

Stop Thief!

By Kim Kimber

Lisa stood very still and listened. Bang! Crash! The sound came again. She hadn't been mistaken. There was someone else in the house and, by the sound of it, they were busily ransacking the lounge.

Removing her shoes, she padded quietly from the bedroom and made her way to the top of the stairs. Thump! Bang! The noises were growing louder. Whoever was downstairs obviously believed that the house was empty.

Peering down the dark stairwell, Lisa saw that the lounge door was open. A single beam of torchlight flashed intermittently across the hall. She considered making a dash for the front door but the hall was long and narrow and the door securely locked from the inside; Lisa had checked it herself.

Her eyes were drawn to the telephone, temptingly positioned on a bookcase near the entrance, but even if she reached it, she would never be able to make a call undetected. Instinctively, Lisa slid her hand in her pocket and felt around for her mobile. Then she remembered, *damn*, she had left it on the kitchen table at her friend Tania's house earlier that day.

Resigning herself to investigating on her own, Lisa made her way silently down the stairs. Reaching the bottom, she peered into the lounge. A dark figure was busily helping himself to the contents of the DVD drawer. *How dare he,* she thought indignantly. Sliding her hand round the door, Lisa fumbled for the light switch and heard a gratifying 'click' as the room was flooded with light.

Rushing in before she had a change of heart, she confronted the intruder. "What do you think you're doing?" she demanded. The thief dropped his bag in fright and turned to face her.

"What does it look like, love," the man growled in a throaty voice, "helping myself aren't I?"

Sizing him up quickly, Lisa realised that he was even smaller than she was. Two black eyes peered out from under a cheap, woollen balaclava. Glancing in the direction of the window which stood half open, she drew herself up to her full 5ft 4in height.

"That's right," the man sneered. "Got in through the window. Didn't anyone ever warn you to lock up when you go out? Wide open it was." As if to illustrate his point, a chilly breeze blew in through the gap, making the curtains dance.

"You can't just break into other people's houses."

"No need to break in. You were asking for it, leaving that window open. A temptation to any passing thief."

"So you thought you'd make off with whatever you fancy," Lisa countered defiantly.

"Why not? You've got so much stuff; you surely won't miss a few trinkets. Now shut up and let me get on or you'll regret it."

"Are you threatening me?"

"And what if I am?" the burglar shouted, lunging towards her in a sudden, swift movement, taking Lisa by surprise. "Who do you think is going to stop me from hurting you?" He grabbed her arm, twisted it behind her back and forced her to the floor. "Now, are you going to be a good girl and sit quietly whilst I finish up here?"

Rubbing her arm and glowering furiously, Lisa nodded.

"Good. That way you won't get hurt."

Turning his back on her, the burglar continued shovelling things into his bag.

Lisa seized her chance. Throwing herself forward, she dived at his legs. Caught off guard, the intruder lost his balance and knocked over an ornamental lamp, sending it crashing to the floor. Acting fast, while he was sprawled in a confused tangle of shattered glass and wire, she bound the burglar's hands behind his back with the cord from the broken lamp.

"Not so menacing now are we?" she said in a satisfied voice, wrenching the balaclava over his head. Without the disguise, he seemed a lot less intimidating. Slightly balding with a bead of sweat on his brow, he looked more comical than fierce.

"Very funny," the thief snarled, struggling in vain to free himself from his bindings.

"You need to be taught a lesson."

"So, what are you going to do?"

Checking her watch, Lisa realised that it was getting late; she really ought to hurry, but the temptation to further humiliate her captive was too great. There was time enough.

"Call the police, what else?"

Going into the hall, she dialled 999. The police arrived at the scene in minutes. Shaking and tearful now that the adrenalin had worn off, Lisa explained what had happened.

"He's in there," she said between sobs, "I surprised him and managed to tie him up. He got in through the window, it was left open I'm afraid."

"Now, miss, it's OK," said one of the police officers reassuringly. "Calm yourself down. We can handle it from here." Lisa smiled weakly and watched as the intruder was escorted to the waiting police car by two burly officers.

"There's been an increase in burglaries in this area lately but thanks to your quick thinking, this chap won't be stealing from anyone else for a while. You'll need to make a statement of course, but as you're obviously very upset, why don't you come down to the station in the morning and we can do it then. I suggest you have a cup of tea and an early night. Is there anyone you would like us to call? You've had quite a shock."

"No, thanks, I'll be fine. My partner should be arriving any moment now."

"If you're sure …" Lisa nodded.

"Well, make sure you lock up properly."

"I wiil, thank you again."

"It's a pleasure. We'll see you in the morning. Oh, and here's the bag we found in the lounge. I think it's full of your property." Lisa took it from the police officer and closed the front door firmly.

Dropping the bag, she ran up the stairs, and made her way to the master bedroom. She had better get a move on; the interruption had cost her valuable time.

Picking up her case, Lisa cast an expert eye over the remaining items of jewellery in the bedroom and dropped them inside.

Slipping on her shoes, she hurried to the front door, carrying the stolen goods and collected the additional bag the police officer had given her. As she reached the pavement a car pulled up alongside her. Lisa threw her case and the bag onto the backseat and jumped in next to the driver.

"Successful night?" asked her accomplice, pulling away from the kerb at speed.

"You could say that," Lisa said smiling. "After all, it's not every day that you get to catch a thief."

My Son is Awfully Grubby

By Debbie Softly

My son is awfully grubby
His father thinks that's good
"A boy should be a boy," he says
But then I guess he would.

My son is awfully grubby
With dirt behind each ear
"There's more to life than washing
mum."
I smile, he's such a dear.

My son is awfully grubby
With trainers old and smelly
Too busy for a shower it seems
Engrossed, in front of telly.

My son is awfully grubby
With muddy football kit
A little soap and water, now
It wouldn't hurt a bit.

My son is awfully grubby
My daughter gives me hope
"Wait till he meets a girl mum,
He'll soon be using soap."

My son is awfully grubby
A girl? I wonder who
I hope it happens soon
You see, my son is 42.

Deeds not Words

By Barbara Sleap

"Are you going to the meeting tonight Em?" Daisy asked her friend as they left the tea room in town, having had tea with some other members of the WSPU.*

"I certainly am Daisy. That new MP is speaking, although I don't suppose he will listen to us any more than the others. I've got my ticket for the floor section; you're in the gallery aren't you? I'm disguising myself this time though, I've borrowed a hat with a black veil and my banner will be tucked into my drawers. I'm getting too well-known these days and if I'm recognised there's bound to be trouble."

"Oh Em, do be careful, you've been arrested twice now. Don't forget the police hurt you last time and prison was so awful for you. We've also got the Derby next week, there's quite a few of us going so we're sure to cause a disturbance. We'll make our presence felt again. One day we'll get that vote, you'll see."

Emily smiled broadly, "Oh yes, I'm looking forward to it and we'll certainly cause a stir Daisy, it should be a worthwhile trip. Perhaps this time they'll sit up and take notice, if not we'll keep on until they do."

Daisy walked home deep in thought. She was worried about Emily who had become, in her opinion, overzealous with the 'votes for women' campaign and her work with the WSPU. Emily had been arrested twice now, once for setting fire to local pillar boxes and again for causing a disturbance at a political rally. Each time she had refused food until she was released, nothing seemed to deter her.

****

One hundred years later Liz sat in her London office staring at her computer screen. She had been tracing her family tree for some time now, it had been a hard task but she had made some surprising discoveries.

It had been a solitary journey; being an only child she had no family to share her findings with. Her grandmother and her father had both died when she was small and her mother had spent her last years in a home suffering from Alzheimer's disease and had died several years earlier.

Now, Liz had just found out that her great-aunt Emily on her mother's side had been an active and well-known member of the suffragette movement, one who had sadly died for the cause. Liz was eager to learn about the life and activities of great-aunt Emily and felt an affinity to the campaign she fought for. Liz had read lots of articles about suffragettes during her time at university and considered these militant ladies, who waged war on conformity, both spirited and courageous, especially at a time when the only opinions women were allowed were what to have for dinner, and how to care for their families, and especially their husbands.

****

The meeting in Newcastle had started well and the new speaker was in full flow, obviously relishing his newly-given power, until Emily, her face hidden by the thick, dark veil stood up, her green, purple and white banner held high while she shouted, "Are you going to give votes to women?" She kept up the chant while others in the gallery loudly followed suit.

The meeting was in turmoil, men shouted insults at the women. Even women were showing their dissent to the activists. The police broke through the now unruly crowd, grabbed Emily and roughly pushed her through the doorway. She fell like a rag doll down several steps where a large assembly of women had gathered in protest. Once again they had caused havoc and made their presence felt but, despite their efforts, few politicians were on their side, in fact there were still women who disagreed with the beliefs of the suffragette movement and disliked the disruption they caused.

Two days later Emily, Daisy and other Union members were on the train heading for Epsom; it hadn't been a straightforward journey so they were tired and hungry. They were all spending the night with members of the Surrey branch, ready for the races taking place the following day.

"There should be a good crowd there tomorrow Daisy," said Emily, "the new London branch is sending a contingency to support us so we'll be well represented. We've got plenty of banners and placards, plus I've got a special plan of my own."

"Oh Em, not again, you'll get into real trouble one day."

"Well I don't care," Emily replied in a stubborn tone, "we must keep on with the fight, it's important Daisy, they can't ignore us forever, it's an injustice. I'm a lawbreaker only to become a lawmaker."

Daisy nodded thoughtfully. Her friend was so passionate about the movement and seemed to have no regard for her own safety, what could she be planning?

****

Liz sat on the train to Northumberland. She was going to find her great-aunt's grave which she had discovered was situated in a churchyard in Morpeth, Emily's hometown, near Newcastle. She had taken two days off from her work merely to satisfy her growing curiosity about Emily. On arrival at Morpeth station she took a taxi and headed for St Mary's Church. On arrival she scanned the many gravestones scattered around the grounds; there seemed a lot for such a small space. Some were well-tended, others unkempt and illegible. She wandered around the deserted yard, trying to be methodical in her search. She had to find it.

****

At the racecourse the minor races were in progress. The atmosphere was lighthearted and the weather fine. The spectators were dressed in their finery, the men in black top hats and tail coats, the ladies in elegant hats and gowns of every colour.

Daisy, Emily and other members of the WSPU moved easily amongst the crowd eagerly waiting for the main race when the King's horse would be running. The plan was to wave placards and unfurl their purple, white and greens at Tattenham corner which they hoped would stop the race. Emily and Daisy moved to the white painted rails to be with the other members.

Daisy looked at Emily who had been very quiet, almost distracted since their arrival at the course. "Are you feeling OK Em?" she asked.

Emily turned to her friend. "I'm fine Daisy; I've had such a lovely day with you all, you've been a good friend to me." She squeezed Daisy's arm just as in the distance the gun went off for the Royal Derby to begin. Daisy could see the horses approaching and felt the pounding beneath her feet. The horses neared and the crowd shouted excitedly, when suddenly Emily slipped under the rail, her placard held high and ran in front of the King's horse which was in the lead.

Daisy called out but her pleas were drowned by the rising euphoria of the crowd. She watched in horror as

Emily fell under the hoofs of the horse and was hurled across the grass and lay still, the horse stumbled and the jockey was thrown onto the ground. Stunned spectators surged onto the course and both Emily and the jockey were picked up and driven by cars to ambulances which ferried them to the nearest hospital. The race had been stopped alright but with harsh consequences.

****

One year later Daisy sat tearfully and contemplated her friend's grave. She tidied away some weeds and placed a small posy down onto the stone. She felt lonely as she sat with her thoughts and memories. Emily's tragic death had been so devastating, she had died two days after the fall but her act had, in a year, caused the politicians to consider the suffragette movement in a more serious vein. The movement, which now had branches all over the country, had caused even more disruption at events and meetings since Emily's death and even more women had endured arrests, prison sentences and hunger strikes.

Women from far and wide had attended Emily's London funeral and had, at the movement's request, arrived garbed in black and carrying purple irises as a mark of respect. Despite lingering animosity, things were beginning to move in the right direction; some MPs were listening although there was still a long haul ahead, and Daisy felt that Emily's death had not been completely in vain. She herself had started to work for the WSPU but she missed her friend so much.

Finally, Daisy stood up and wiped away her tears, she smiled fondly at her friend's memorial. Emily would have been very proud.

****

Liz moved from one side of the church to the other and was surprised to see there ahead of her the grave of Emily Davison surrounded by railings to highlight its importance. She entered by the ornate iron gate and read the engraving, *'Deeds not Words'*. She felt a deep empathy with her unknown ancestor and sat in contemplation for a short while before tidying some of the weeds surrounding the stone. She laid down a small posy and shed a tear for great-aunt Emily whose actions had helped to bring the ideas and opinions of women to the fore.

Eventually, Liz got up, dried her eyes and smiled fondly at the grave. Perhaps her aunt would have been proud of what she herself had achieved in her role as a solicitor specialising in women's rights and issues? With her head held high she walked back to the waiting taxi. Yes, Emily would have been very proud.

*WSPU Women's Social and Political Union
Founded in 1898 by Emmeline Pankhurst

Evening

By Trisha Todd

It's twilight, the pale blue memory of day fading as it chases the sun westwards and into night. The streetlights are awakening, glowing embers against the darkening sky. The house is still and silent, breath held until the children return. It's a rare occasion and I'm keen to take advantage of this infrequent lull.

I ignore the debris in the kitchen, the fallout from this evening's dinner, the aroma following me as I head upstairs to the quiet sanctuary of my bedroom - but I am not alone. As I close the door and turn, he is there. His eyes stare into mine, his desire plain to see within their molten caramel depths. Though no words are spoken, I know what he wants immediately.

I reach for him, wanting to run my fingers through his hair. It used to be longer, curling loosely all over, but has since been trimmed and just edges over his collar. I wonder again at the different shades and textures; coarse gingerbread fading to pale honey where it covers his ears. It is softer there, silken and smooth against my fingertips.

Impatient, he nudges me. It's difficult to resist him, but I tell him to wait; I'm not ready for him yet.

His long legs seemingly too slender to support him, he sprawls possessively across the bed, filling the space with his powerful frame. I lean over him to caress his barrel chest, stroking the hair there, and he edges closer playfully, his hot, wet tongue flicking out against the end of my nose. Laughing, I know I can't put him off too much longer, and he sits up expectantly.

Finally surrendering, I get his lead and take Scooby out for his evening walk.

The Craic

By Sandra Casey

Roisin recalls a funny incident, while having a cup of tea with her friend. She talks to Mary about a time when a young English couple stayed in her B&B, just outside Kilkenny, Ireland.

"They were a lovely couple, they were!"

"Where from?"

"Oh English like. London, I tink?"

"Pass me the tea, Roisin. What happened then?"

"There's jam for the scones. Don't have too much cream Mary! The call was in the afternoon. I was having me nap."

"Stttttt!"

"Oh I don't mind like. She was very polite. Very English like and asked if I had a room. They were driving around from Cork and flying back out of Kilkenny."

"Oh aye."

"So I gave them the tea and scones, and showed them the Rose room with the single and the double. Such a lovely couple, I dropped them off in town on the tear."

"Oh that was good of you, Roisin!"

"Aye. Well. I might have scared them running a few lights mind. Her face was white as a sheet sitting in the back"

"Ha ha ha."

"Anyways, I heard them come in like a herd of elephants. She banned him to the single cos he'd had too much plain and was acting the maggot."

"The oaf!"

"Next thing I heard this bang. The door flung open! For a moment in my sleep I thought Paddy had come back from the dead!"

"Jesus, Mary and Joseph!"

"I opened me eyes at the clock and it was about three, and then nearly fell out of me bed! Your man is standing in me room, all six feet, completely in the nip! Before I could do anything about it, he was off down the stairs and out of the front door."

"Holy show, Roisin! Was he looking for the jacks?"

"Aye. Oh it was a gas, Mary! By the time I had my gown on he was back up the stairs. Gave me a fright. Many a time I had to run down that path to fetch Paddy back from the main road!"

"And where was your woman, all this time?"

"Oh, didn't have a clue! I had to tell her when she came down for breakfast. Nearly choked on her egg!"

Lucy

By Josephine Gibson

It was the early mornings that Lucy liked the best. Her breasts would be full of milk and Amy would feed smoothly and efficiently, her eyes closed, her focus purely on the warm, life-giving flow. Lucy felt so proud of sustaining her daughter, delighting in her chubby thighs and showering her round tummy with kisses as she changed her nappy. Afterwards she would rock Amy back to sleep as she stood at the window and watched the sky change from grey to pink.

She would listen to Josh's quiet breathing, knowing that as she climbed back into bed he would reach out for her and she would welcome his sleepy hardness. She was mother, she was woman, she had everything she needed. She revelled in Josh's firm muscles and he in her soft, maternal body; they shared a mutual amazement at the satisfaction each could bring the other. After he had finished and it was her turn, he would sometimes come up for air and playfully blow a raspberry on her tummy feeling, she assumed, the joyfulness with which she had kissed Amy. They would collapse in giggles together, increasing to snorting through their noses and burying their heads under the pillows, when they heard Lucy's mother stirring and preparing for her day.

No longer for them furtive encounters in cars, in spare rooms at parties, in long desperate walks through scrubland searching for privacy. No, they had inherited Annette's room when Amy was born because Lucy's had been too small for a cot, and so they were determined to make the bed their own.

It had all seemed such a disaster when Lucy realised she was pregnant. Annette had thought she had so carefully protected Lucy from repeating her own mistakes: the serious and excruciating talks about contraception, the watchfulness whenever Josh visited, the beating of breasts and sharing of her litany of disastrous men. As if Lucy cared!

"Mum, I know you feel sad about what's happened in your life, but I'm not you. I'm not gonna make the same mistakes – I know what I'm doing mum."

"Lucy, I know you think you do, but I'm your mum and what I'm saying..."

"I know what you're saying mum! Bo-ring! I can handle myself, OK?"

And she would scoot out, in her little skirt, and her kitten heels, and push herself against Josh in a dark corner because she was 16, she had her whole life in front of her and she'd be damned if she spent it at home with a mother with a long face and a history.

It was a bit of a come down to admit she was pregnant.

But she soon found herself in a group of the 'naughty girls' who looked out for each other as their pregnancies progressed, giggling at the middle-aged midwives and their variety of instruments for labour: hooks and cups and tongs, needles and tubes, cold gel for the tummy, sonic aid for the mysteriously fast heartbeat. The breastfeeding class was a hoot, the midwife spluttering over a knitted breast when Lucy cracked a joke about her using it to keep a man warm in winter.

Lucy felt proud, in this group of ne'er-do-wells, that she had a man who was sticking with her. A real man, 18-years-old, who was giving up his plans to study and had already found a job so he could support her and the baby. She could hold her head up and talk about what she was buying for her baby, what names Josh liked, how many kids they might have together. Not for her the indignity of relying on grandma to buy a buggy. She was a mature woman who could advise the other girls on their relationships - and in that moment forget the sight of Josh's mother, standing at her door with silent tears, watching Josh leave home to live with his pregnant girlfriend. Stupid, stuck-up woman anyway, with her false smile and her family photographs, her certificates on the wall, her denial that Lucy was important to Josh. As if he'd want to leave Lucy and Amy to go to university.

It was a terrible shock when he did.

And in that moment, when Annette returned from work, and found Lucy white-faced and sobbing, clutching her daughter, there was no anger. There was tea, an appropriation of her granddaughter, and a sense of resignation.

"Well, Lucy, what do you think you're going to do now?"

"Oh mum, I don't know, I suppose I'll have to look at college. The clinic told us about some courses, childcare and that. I know you found it tough being a single mum, and you wished you'd done better."

"That's right. I hated not having a decent job and having to rely on your dad for handouts - not that he ever really helped."

Lucy sipped her tea and looked at Amy reaching up to touch her grandmother's face. She noticed how Annette's eye shadow had settled into the creases formed through years of work and worry. She thought of her mother sitting at the kitchen table, pen in hand, carefully unfolding and counting £20 notes, accounting for what she had earned and what she had spent. She remembered packing their bags and moving between numerous flats, the men who had come and gone until Annette had declared, "That is it! No more!" and how their lives had settled down until she, as a teenager, had decided it was time to bring boys home. Suddenly the image of her and Josh giggling in Annette's bed returned, bringing a sick feeling to her stomach.

"I'll take Amy now, mum. You go off and have your bath. I thought I'd cook tonight."

She stroked the fine, blonde curls that were forming on Amy's head, kissed her and breathed in a deep smell of baby. Nothing had changed. She was still mother – and daughter. She came from strong stock, from family who knew how to survive, women who could get by.

"Mum!" she called. "Could you sit tonight? No point me staying at home getting miserable, is there?"

Your Country Needs You!

By Karen Richardson

The heat of the June day was dissipating when I rode my bicycle away from York, my previous life, and on towards the River Ouse. I needed solitude to calm my feelings and knew that being near the river was my best hope to get that.

Despite the perfect summer weather, I was right in my assumption that I would not have company or anyone watching my movements by the river. Children were probably running errands for their parents before enjoying a well-earned couple of hours to play in the street. The freight barges which travelled daily along the Ouse to Hull had finished work for the day. I guessed too that even clerks from the main Post Office, where I had worked for over 12 years, would not bother to venture out here either, midweek after work. The local pubs had always been a more likely haunt for them.

There weren't so many lads working in the Post Office alongside me now. They had been replaced by middle-aged men and young lasses eager to earn a good, regular wage away from the Rowntree factory and get the chance of bettering themselves in the process. The lads who had joined the Post Office with me straight from school, had disappeared in the late summer of 1914, when the first rush of patriotic enthusiasm had seen the majority of them sign up for war and adventure faster than the ink could dry on their recruitment forms.

I left my bicycle by the railings next to the riverbank and, in a fit of youthful exuberance, I climbed one of the sycamore trees. As I made myself comfortable on the wide branch, I had plenty of time to think about how my whole life had disintegrated in less than two years.

I certainly had a loving family upbringing, but my father had been killed in 1901 during the Boer War. He had been a career soldier and had embodied the *Boy's Own* magazine type of manliness. Despite that loss, I had still done very well for myself at school and my mother was immensely proud of me when I started as a messenger boy at the main Post Office in York, close to home. I had my doubts whether she would be so proud of me now and my father would have never tolerated my conchie views.

I felt that the entire world had gone mad and that it had been against me for months. Mother had tried her best to support and understand my point of view on the war, but I had known that our neighbours, the church congregation and her friends had all snubbed her. I had been verbally attacked by complete strangers and maligned daily by the military and newspaper campaigns to coerce, and then force men, into joining up.

I knew that my stance as a conscientious objector would be unpopular, but I felt as a socialist, that if the workers of all countries united and refused to fight, that there would be no war. I believed that the working class of this country had no argument with the working class of Germany or anywhere else in the world.

I was a minority within the types of conscientious objectors. There were a higher number of religious objectors and I felt that they were slightly better tolerated by the public, rather than the men like me who had objected because of political or socialist beliefs. I was viewed as both a crank and a shirker.

I knew that my rights and freedom were being inched away as each month of the war had gone by. Asquith and his government had been single-minded in bringing in the Military Service Act at the start of 1916, despite their previous promises, in order to conscript all remaining men between the ages of 18 and 41 to fight. I was certain that their net would be cast ever wider, as they needed more and more men at the Front. The casualty lists had been published in the newspapers over the past year and the losses had horrified me.

I appeared in front of our local tribunal in April to be faced by a panel of nine closed-minded bigots, who took great delight in humiliating me and stamping down my reasons for exemption. My hearing had barely lasted five minutes. I had applied for absolutist exemption, as I didn't wanted to be involved on any level in the war. I opposed conscription utterly and refused to take part in any work directly or indirectly involved with the war. I told the tribunal panel that I was a committed objector. The serving officer on the panel was the worst of all of them, and he had questioned my right to call myself a real man. I applied for an appeal against their decision that I was to be drafted into Kitchener's army, but I started to feel the desperation and fear creep through my body as I waited each day for the notification of the appeal tribunal date to be set.

By the time that date arrived, I doubted, harangued and berated myself continually. If other men could undertake what I had refused to do, was I wrong in my beliefs after all? There had been so much pressure against conscientious objectors for such a long time. I wondered, when the war ever ended, what else I would have had to face from the men coming back. Or from the wives of the men who wouldn't ever return. I had seen the soldiers in York who had been invalided out with a Blighty wound. I continually felt like a leper.

Had there been the slightest disappointment and shame in my mother's eyes as well? She wished me luck as I set out this morning for the appeal tribunal, dressed in my best suit and spotlessly polished boots. I was undecided when I placed two letters in my suit pocket; one was my appeal tribunal notification and the other an apology and explanation for mother.

I was mentally exhausted when I finally reached my decision, although in reality my choice had been made for me by others.

I reassured myself that the letters in my suit pocket were secure as I unfastened my trouser braces. My letter for mother was the most important as, even at that late stage, I still wanted her to know that I wished the circumstances could have been different. The appointment letter for my tribunal was superfluous now.

I was always a fastidious type of fellow and so wanted a clean and tidy conclusion. My braces coiled as tightly around the sycamore tree branch as they did around my neck.

My beliefs were never going to be considered valid within the machinery of war.

My life was my own to take.

The Wives of Henry VIII

By Barbara Sleap

Catherine of Aragon was Henry's first wife
From Spain she came to start a new life.
After twenty-four years Henry changed his course
And he and Catherine got a divorce.

Anne Boleyn was Henry's next thought
But she was not liked by the men of the court.
She was put on trial, or so it is said
They found her guilty so off with her head!

Jane Seymour was to be Henry's next queen
And to have a son Henry was keen.
So Jane gave him Edward, an heir he was told
But poor Jane died when he was two weeks old.

Anne of Cleves from Europe came next
But living in England made her vexed.
So six months later came another divorce
To make way for wife number five of course!

Katherine Howard was a lively young girl
Who put poor old Henry's life in a whirl,
But she made friends with men just after they wed
So the axe man chopped off another wife's head.

For wife number six Henry did not look too far
At Hampton Court Palace he wed Katherine Parr.
But before he got to chop off her head
In 1547 poor Henry was dead.

Where Do You Go, StevieMo?

By Lois Maulkin

In the last chance half hour between tea and bedtime, StevieMo, eight-years-old with blonde hair and just a few freckles, headed out to play. He ran to the shed at the end of the garden path where his bike, a yellow chopper, was kept. A blackbird was singing.

As his hand touched the shed door, the light seemed to flicker, just for a moment. A slight chill made him shiver, and StevieMo felt a tiny bit afraid of... something... no, nothing. He was fine, he told himself. Everything was fine. He pulled open the shed door, perhaps a little more slowly than usual, but everything inside was just as it always was – just the same, the grass-and-oil smell of the mower, and there were the shears, wrapped in a really dirty tea-towel that his mum said was as old as the hills. StevieMo sometimes wondered about that. He knew that the hills were old enough to have dinosaur fossils in, so were at least as old as dinosaurs, and he thought tea-towels came into existence later than dinosaurs. Anyway, he couldn't imagine dinosaurs using tea-towels, not with those tiny little arms.

His bike was leaning against his old folded pushchair and a fireguard, and StevieMo stepped into the shed towards it, but as he did so, everything suddenly felt very strange indeed. His bike seemed to be disappearing into the distance, shrinking and fading, and StevieMo found himself falling, down, and down, and still further down, as the shed floor shuddered beneath his feet and then wasn't there at all. The light was being sucked out of the open door, somewhere above his head, and there was a smell like used fireworks, and StevieMo opened his mouth to shout *'mum!'* but no sound came out, no sound at all, and the darkness rushed into him...

He awoke to hear a boy's voice saying "Are you all right?" and found he was lying at the foot of a huge old apple tree in the corner of a field he didn't recognise. The boy, who was a little grubby, was wearing some very long grey shorts and holding a homemade bow and some arrows. He was standing over him looking concerned. "Did it hit you?" he asked.

"Pardon?" said StevieMo, standing up carefully, and brushing off a huge quantity of blossom.

"My arrow," said the boy. "I was aiming at a blackbird on that branch up there, and I shot towards it, only the blackbird flew away and you fell out. I didn't realise it was such a good arrow." StevieMo wasn't quite sure how he had got to be where he was. The boy seemed friendly, and StevieMo found there was something very comforting about looking at him, so he was not feeling afraid, just slightly confused.

"What's your name?" asked the boy.

"StevieMo," said StevieMo. "Who are you?"

"I'm the Lone Ranger," said the boy with a grin, "so you'll have to be Tonto. Come on Tonto, the Indians are just over the hill! Hi Ho Silver!" and he galloped off across the field on an imaginary horse, with StevieMo running after him. At the hedge, the Lone Ranger dismounted elaborately and lay down on the ground. "Get down, Tonto, my faithful companion!" he hissed, and StevieMo dropped onto his belly. The two boys crawled, commando-like, towards a stile set in the hedge. "Ready?" asked the boy. StevieMo nodded, and they peered over the stile together.

A group of elegantly dressed men, in swishy capes and breeches and pointed boots with silvery buckles were striding about in the next field. They were taking things out of the inside pockets in their capes. One pulled out a rippling tangle of sparkling necklaces, and held them up proudly. Another pulled out fistfuls of golden coins, which he trickled from hand to hand. Another held up a massive jar of sherbet pips.

"They're not Indians," exclaimed StevieMo, "they're robbers! Highwaymen!"

"Quiet," hissed the Lone Ranger out of the corner of his mouth. "They're plotting something. That one with the purple waistcoat, he's Dick Turnip, the chief, and he's the most dangerous one. We need to hear what he's saying."

Dick Turnip spoke boldly, and conveniently loudly; "Soon we must attack."

StevieMo and the Lone Ranger looked at each other in shock.

There were murmurs of "Yes, good idea!" from the other highwaymen.

"As you know, we usually attack at night, so attacking in the daytime gives us the element of surprise. The sun's just about to go down, so we're already a bit late. Let's get on our trusty steeds and get started!"

A stampede of wild horses, their manes and tails flying behind them and their heads tossing proudly, burst out from behind a tree, galloped up and circled once or twice, and then slowed to let the highwaymen jump on to them. They turned, whinnying and rearing, towards the stile where StevieMo and the Lone Ranger crouched, watching. And then... and then they came. The earth shook with the drumming of hooves. The air was filled with aristocratic laughter, pistol shots and the rattling of the massive bottle of sherbet pips. The horses were coming, coming, coming. StevieMo felt he was going to be sick. He was certain they would both be trampled, certain he would never see his mum or dad again. His heart was thudding. He wanted to run away, but as hard as he tried he couldn't make his legs move.

The Lone Ranger said "Don't worry Tonto! I've got my bow; all I need to do is shoot Dick Turnip. Without him they're useless."

"Then shoot him!" squeaked StevieMo. "Quick!"

The horses were nearing the edge of the field now, and some of them had taken off and were rising in graceful arcs over the hedge. StevieMo held his breath as one sailed over his head. He shut his eyes and tried to shout "Quickly, please, quickly!" but could only manage a whisper.

There was a twanging sound, and the whizz of an arrow in flight, and a pattering sound as sherbet pips rained down on them.

"It's all right now, Tonto, we're safe! And look at all these sweets!"

StevieMo opened his eyes. He was alone in the field with the boy, who was picking sherbet pips out of the grass. "Where are the highwaymen? And the horses?" he asked, getting shakily to his feet.

"Gone," said the boy simply. "I shot Dick Turnip and they've gone. We're on velvet. Want some of these?" He held out a fistful of tiny sweets, and said "I haven't had sweets for ages. If mum's got the coupons there are none in the shops." His voice sounded wobbly for a moment, and then he wiped his eyes roughly, and said determinedly "What shall we play now? You choose."

"Play?" said StevieMo, suddenly feeling more relieved and happy than he could ever remember feeling before. It was all play! He put some sherbet pips (three yellows and a pink) into his mouth, and some (five pinks, a yellow and four whites) in his pocket for later. "Play? Pirates, of course!"

"Watch out, then!" said the boy, holding up an imaginary telescope and scanning the opposite edge of the field. "They're coming! Look, they're on the Titanic!"

StevieMo stared in amazement as an enormous ship, bigger than a house, slid silently along behind the hedge. It had masts and fluttering sails on the top, and bristled with cannons.

"It doesn't look like the Titanic," said StevieMo.

"That's because the pirates have captured it and made it their own. It's a pirate ship now. It's got the Jolly Roger on and everything. And here come the pirates!"

As StevieMo watched, dozens of ropes unfurled down the sides of the ship and men with eye patches, men with ear-rings, men with beards of many colours, men with striped trousers, men with wooden legs, men with tricorn hats and flocks of parrots circling them began to descend. StevieMo could hear the parrots squawking, the *"ho, ho, ho, me hearties!"* cries of the pirates, and the clanging of their wooden legs against the metal sides of the Titanic.

"Are they coming for us?" said StevieMo, pleased to notice he felt quite brave about the whole situation.

"Yes," said the boy. "But it's all right. We can get on that whale over there and escape. Come on!"

A fountain of earth sprayed into the air to the left of the two boys, and they ran over to where a great, glistening, grey whale had burst up out of the grass and was swimming happily through the turf. They climbed up the sides of the whale - it obligingly dipped down into the earth to let them do so a lot more easily than you might have imagined. They sat on its massive head, holding on with their knees and balancing with outstretched arms. "Right, off we go!" said the boy, and the whale shot off, with the Titanic following.

StevieMo's hair blew out behind him and flicked in his eyes as he looked back to check the distance between the whale and the Titanic. "It's gaining on us!" he cried. "We need an iceberg to frighten it away!" Luckily, at that moment, the tip of an iceberg, about the size and shape of a very pointy cabbage, came into view and the whale headed towards it.

"Grab it!" shouted StevieMo. The whale sunk low into the earth and the boy leaned out to hook his bow around the tip of the iceberg. "Got it!" he cried, "let's give the Titanic what for!" and the whale turned round and headed, slowly (icebergs are REALLY big below the surface and REALLY heavy to drag) towards the Titanic. The iceberg shone in the evening sun, and as it began to follow them across the field, twinkles of reflected yellow light shot out of it and struck many of the pirates in their remaining good eyes, and sent several of them scurrying back up the ropes. Then the Titanic itself, realising an iceberg was heading its way, began to shiver and shudder in fright and the ropes hanging down its sides began to jiggle and flick about, with the pirates jiggling and flicking about on the ends. The pirates shouted rude words and tried to shake their fists but didn't dare let go of their ropes, and the massive ship turned quickly, blasting its horn in panic, and set off, full steam ahead, away over the horizon.

The boys cheered, and thanked the whale for its help by posting sherbet pips (two whites, two pinks), down its blowhole. It swam off gracefully, leaping in and out of the furrows and tufts of grass in elegant display.

"What now?" asked StevieMo. "Aeroplanes?" He stuck his arms out and set off across the field at a run, the boy following behind, laughing.

"I'm a spitfire!" shouted the boy. "What are you?"

"Concorde," said StevieMo.

The boy stopped running, looking worried. "You're what?" he asked. "Is that foreign? You're not the Bosch, are you?"

"It's French, I think," said StevieMo, stopping too.

"That's velvet!" said the boy with a grin, adjusting imaginary goggles. "Got your parachute? Chocks away!" and he stuck out his arms again and trotted off. Making a droning noise, the boys ran across the field a short way and then, to StevieMo's amazement, he realised that his feet, although still running, were no longer touching the ground, and he was rising higher and higher into the air. To the side of him, he could see the Spitfire had also taken off and was laughing with delight.

"Right, Concorde," said the Spitfire, "we've got to hide in the sun, so we can fly out of it again when the enemy planes come over, and give them a jolly good surprise."

"OK," said StevieMo, banking to get into the right position. Looking down, he could see fields and trees and then parts of the town. He was clearing the roofs of houses easily. He was higher than the steeples. And he could see his father, distinctive in his policeman's uniform, walking along the high street on his way home.

"There's my dad! Dad!" he shouted. As if he had heard, StevieMo's dad turned, smiling and looked in his direction. StevieMo waved, but his dad didn't wave back, he just carried on walking, and smiling. And suddenly, for a tiny moment, StevieMo wanted very much to go home, but he had no idea how to get there.

"Never mind your dad!" shouted the Spitfire, "there's the enemy at two o'clock! Ready?" Suddenly, a flock of what looked at first like birds appeared out of nowhere, racing towards the Spitfire and Concorde. The enemy planes were silent, their engine noise flew away behind them, and they loomed menacingly, growing larger and larger as they neared. Then, hundreds of little red lights started fizzing from them.

"Shoot back at them!" cried the Spitfire, making fists with his hands and jabbing with his thumbs and shouting "ack, ack, ack," as loudly as he could. StevieMo did the same, jabbing and yelling, and one by one the enemy planes dropped out of the sky, fluttering and twisting down onto the town. Small figures parachuted out and drifted across the town like dandelion seeds, blowing away, far over the horizon. The planes hit the ground with an incredibly loud crunching sound, and flames and smoke shot up from the buildings they landed on and turned to ruins.

As the last enemy plane went down, the Spitfire let out a whoop of triumph, and flew a victory roll in the air 50 feet above the smouldering remains of the Bata Shoes factory. "What a dogfight!" he shouted in glee. StevieMo looked down with horror at the demolished buildings, the glowing flames and the eddying smoke. He was hugely relieved to see his dad was still walking home at the same leisurely pace, although much of the town behind him had disintegrated.

The two planes turned back and started their descent into the field. As they landed, StevieMo said "I should be going back home." It was much darker now, and StevieMo sniffed to see whether the air was full of smoke or twilight. No smoky smell, he was relieved to notice, but that meant it was dark because it was late, and he might even have missed bath time.

"Can you come again tomorrow? I haven't got anyone else to play with," said the boy, picking up his arrows from the ground near the stile. "Have you got time for one last game?"

"I don't think so. I really must get home. It's so late. And I don't know where my house is from here. I think I'm going to be in trouble. I have to be in before my dad gets home, and he might even be there now."

"You need a time machine," said the boy. They had walked along the hedge to a tree with a hole in it, and the boy reached his hand in and pulled out a tea-towel with Southend Pier embroidered on it, and wrapped his bow and arrows in it, quite carefully. As he looked at the tea-towel, StevieMo had a very strange feeling. It was the kind of feeling you get when you are trying to remember a dream you had the night before, and you concentrate really hard and for an instant you are certain you are about to remember it, but it slips away again, swallowed into the darkness at the very back of your mind.

"Sorry," said StevieMo, shaking his head a little, "what did you say?"

"I said you need a time machine," said the boy, putting the tea-towel bundle back into the hollow. "Then you could get home an hour ago!"

"Yes, I need a TARDIS!" said StevieMo.

The boy looked blankly at him.

"You know, a TARDIS, like on *Dr Who*. You must know!" insisted StevieMo. "Inside it's huge, with a massive control panel and Dr Who and his assistant press all the buttons, and go travelling through space and time, and outside, well outside, it looks a bit like a telephone box."

A smile spread across the boy's face.

"What?" he asked, pointing to the corner of the field, "like that one there?" And there, in all its shiny scarlet glory, at the point where two hedges met, was a telephone box. It was a little unusual, as yellow flowered curtains were hung across its glass so you couldn't see inside it. A blackbird sat on the top, singing into the twilight.

The boys ran over. As they neared it, the telephone box seemed to shimmer a little, like an oasis of water in the road on a hot day, and StevieMo thought *'it's not really there'*. But it was there. They stood and looked at it for a few moments, and StevieMo thought he could hear noises coming from inside and felt a little nervous.

"Go on, then," said the boy. "Go in!"

"I didn't see it before," said StevieMo, trying not to let his voice tremble.

"It wasn't here before," said the boy. "It's come travelling through space and time to take you home. Quick, get in before the tiger gets you!"

"What tiger?" asked StevieMo.

Following the boy's pointing finger, StevieMo could see a jungle growing steadily across the field. Ranks of immense trees, with vines and creepers hanging from them and meshing them densely together, were shooting, with a rustling kind of popping sound, out of the field into the dusky sky. Snakes' tongues could be seen, quite clearly, licking out of the tree tops, tasting the evening. The air was full of the whoops of monkeys, the snarling of hidden beasts and the smell of damp budgerigars. The jungle kept flinging itself up, row upon row, nearer and nearer, and the roaring grew louder and louder.

"Hurry!" said the boy.

StevieMo took the deepest breath he had ever taken, deeper even than when mum rinsed the shampoo from his hair, took two steps forward, and pulled open the telephone box door. He looked inside, and laughed with disbelief.

"They're here!" yelled the boy. "The tigers! Quick!" and he shoved StevieMo into the telephone box and slammed the door shut behind him. StevieMo stumbled and fell forwards into the darkness, landing awkwardly on his bike, he knocked the fireguard over, and the folded pushchair. The door was pulled open again, quite suddenly, and there stood his mum.

"StevieMo, what on earth are you doing?" she asked, taking his hand and helping him up. He could smell the lawnmower, and hear a blackbird singing. "Have you been hiding in there all the time? Come up for your bath now; dad'll be home any minute."

Later on, as his dad was eating his dinner and StevieMo sat at the kitchen table in his dressing gown having a glass of milk, his dad asked "what did you get up to today, then? Out on your bike with Sam, were you?"

StevieMo shook his head.

"No," he said, "I played with someone else today."

"Oh? Who was that?" asked his dad, stirring his tea.

"The Lone Ranger," said StevieMo.

His dad grinned. "I used to play that game when I was a little boy," he said. "So did you have to be Tonto?"

StevieMo nodded.

"I was always the Lone Ranger," said his dad, in a remembering kind of way. "It was when we were all sent out to the countryside in the war. I lived out on a farm and none of the other evacuees lived nearby. I had to pretend I had a friend to be my Tonto."

"Ah, your famous imaginary friend!" said StevieMo's mum.

His dad laughed and said "He was very real to me! It's funny he should come up tonight. I was thinking about him this evening on my way home."

"What was he like?" asked StevieMo.

"Blonde hair and freckles, just like you," said his dad, leaning back in his chair, and winking at StevieMo's mum. "That's why you're called StevieMo, because you reminded me of him from the minute you were born, and that was his name. Did I never tell you that?"

StevieMo shook his head. There was a strange, scratchy feeling at the back of his neck, and a prickly feeling in his eyes, and a tear trickled down his cheek. He wiped it away with the cuff of his dressing gown, and his voice was small and croaky as he said "I went somewhere else in the shed today. There were fields, with whales and spitfires and pirates and things. And he talked about velvet."

His dad looked at him thoughtfully. StevieMo thought he might be cross, and start asking a lot of questions that he wouldn't be able to answer, but his dad just said, quite gently, "You all right?"

StevieMo nodded. "It was fun, but I feel a bit strange now."

His dad went out to the shed *'just to have a little look'*, and his mum took StevieMo upstairs, saying he was tired and had an overactive imagination and was *'exactly the same as his dad, only ever-so-slightly worse'*. As he closed the curtains, StevieMo looked out of his window at the town, where everything was as it should be, with no flames or sirens or flashing emergency lights. StevieMo's mum tucked him into bed and folded his clothes away. She picked up his jeans, and some sherbet pips (a pink, two whites and a yellow), fell out of the pocket.

His dad came up the stairs, whistling the theme from the Lone Ranger. StevieMo felt safe and sleepy and snuggled down into his bed, and heard his dad saying "I found this on the shed floor. Haven't seen it for years!"

"It must have fallen off the shears," said StevieMo's mum. "Goodness it's filthy, let me wash it," and she held out her hand to take it, the ancient tea-towel embroidered with Southend Pier.

Dating Game

A Short Play

By Lynda Brown

Empty stage except for two chairs at the front, facing the audience.

Girl walks on from stage left. Goes directly to the nearest chair and places her bag on the floor to her left.

Boy enters stage right. He looks nervous. Gradually makes his way to the other chair.

Dialogue is directed at the audience.

Girl:	Hi!
Boy:	Oh – hi!
Girl:	Julia.
Boy:	Simon.
Girl:	First time?
Boy:	Yeah! You?
Girl:	Second time here. Been to the one in the High Street a few times.
Boy:	Which one is better?
Girl:	Drinks are cheaper here *(laughs)*.

Boy: *(Forced laugh.)*

Pause

Girl: Now you ask what I do.
Boy: Hmm? Oh, what do you do?
Girl: I'm a masseur.
Boy: *(Sits up.)* Yeah?
Girl: Nah, hairdresser but we have the chairs
          that give you a massage while we're
          washing yer hair. What do you do?
Boy: I'm an actor.
Girl: Nah!
Boy: Yeah! Got me Equity card and
          everything.
Girl: What yer bin in?
Boy: I'm in the latest Bond movie.
Girl: Naaah!
Boy: Yeah – boy walking down the street,
          scene 32 and body to the left of bridge,
          scene 75.

(Sound of bell ringing.)

Boy: What's that?
Girl: Time's up. You have time to get a drink,
          have a pee and then do it all over again

with the next one. I'm 23 on yer list.
You're my number one *(winks)*.

Boy: Oh!

Girl: Bye for now.

Boy: Yeah – bye!

(Girl bends down to pick up a bag. At the same time the boy looks for something in his right hand pocket. Their eyes meet.)

Girl: Hi! I'm Julia.

Boy: Simon.

(Lights fade.)

Calvi

By Sandra Casey

My chin rests on my arm as I look out of the window, the grooves of the old wooden train door digging tracks into the surface of my skin. I close my eyes and raise my head towards the sun, feeling a sparkling array of hot spokes beaming down on my face.

I can smell salty air and dry arid plants, a familiar heady scent of Mediterranean climes and the faint, sweet, coconut and lime of my sun cream, defending me from the penetrating rays.

I hear pockets of chatter like a family of squirrels in a tree, excited passengers, in wonder at the beauty as we turn the corner of each bay and discover the iridescent cobalt and aquamarine inlets, dressed with golden sand dunes and freckled with wild and unforgiving rocks. Protecting the land, providing safe harbours for the young, as they scour them for treasures of the sea.

She is an old train; she looks tired from her many journeys but she has a rich aroma and wraps you in her velvety arms, like a mother with her young. She takes care, pulling slowly into each platform to carefully unload her delicate cargo safely.

She whispers a farewell to me now. As we draw near to my station, she sighs and we roll into a gentle stop. My feet touch the platform, higher than the dunes, but it is still covered in rolling swathes of glistening tiny white diamond pieces of sand. The brightness hurts my eyes and I clothe them with my dark sunglasses and make my way down to the beach.

The sand weighs heavy on my feet like Dutch wooden clogs, as I trudge past the beach hut cafes, weaving through the striped umbrellas with little feet poking out. Still, lifeless bodies lay beneath them worshipping the shafts of light smiling down on them.

As I reach the shore the sand is wet and hard. I run to the water's edge, hopping from one foot to the other to escape the pain from the heat underfoot. It's as though I am walking on hundreds of shards of glass, making little incisions in my soles.

I feel the water around my ankles and the pain has gone. The sea is clear as crystal. I wiggle my toes and watch the little fish dart here and there. I feel calm and relaxed as I walk back onto the beach and up and over to the dunes.

Winding in and out of the dunes, the path suddenly flattens and I pick up my feet. The ground, a river of cinnamon and nutmeg, crunches underfoot; the years of fallen pine needles, laying a bed of minute daggers, happy to spear blood from the inexperienced.

It is cool and dark here. I am sheltered from the heat of the day. I take a moment to breathe in the fresh, chilled air. Silence. I could stand here forever but my back is hot and wet where the backpack lays heavy on my shoulders. I can see the arch through the trees now.

A *'welcome home'* sign could not be better. A bubble of joy works up through my body as my step quickens.

I make my way to the small wooden summerhouse by the side of the arch. Still painted grey-white like I remember. Paint slowly peeling and flaking from the wood. As I approach I can see Papa Pinede through the window. A short, wide jolly man with dark hair and curly moustache like Napoleon Bonaparte himself. He smiles out to me and calls "Bonjour Mademoiselle Anglais, you are home again."

Yes. I am home again.

Weight Watching

By Kim Kimber

"Take off your shoes and step onto the scales." They are out. The words I have been dreading. I fiddle with the laces on my trainers, avoiding the moment for as long as possible. The doctor peers over the top of her glasses impatiently, "Leave them on if it's easier."

One quick tug on each foot and my trainers hit the floor with a gentle thud, sounding as heavy as I feel.

"Should I take my socks off as well? They must weigh a few pounds," I ask optimistically.

"No, your shoes will suffice."

There is no escape. Gingerly, I step on to the scales of doom and close my eyes, not daring to confront the horrible truth.

"Twelve stone, thirteen pounds," the doctor announces triumphantly. "Slip your shoes back on and sit down."

I wince as the reality sinks in; I weigh nearly thirteen stone. I slump into the chair opposite the doctor, feeling like a naughty school child awaiting punishment.

"Well, you do seem to have gained weight rather rapidly, which might account for the breathlessness and dizzy spells. Has there been any change to your diet recently?"

"Chocolate orange," I mumble uncomfortably, shuffling in my seat.

"I beg your pardon, chocolate what?"

"Orange. I just can't seem to get enough. It started small with just one segment at a time, then a whole orange and now it's got to the stage where I can get through five or six a day."

The doctor removes her glasses, places them on the desk and gives me her full attention. "Five or six? That's a lot of calories and very little nutritional value. What else do you eat during an average day?"

"I have three meals; breakfast, lunch and dinner," I say brightly. Surely that has to count for something?

"Talk me through a typical day's eating."

"I have a cup of coffee in the morning…"

"With milk and sugar?" the doctor interrupts.

"Milk, no sugar, and a chocolate orange…"

"For breakfast? No toast or cereal?"

"Err, no."

"Chocolate is not a proper meal," the doctor says, tapping on the computer keyboard in front of her. "Please continue."

"I have a sandwich for lunch – chicken or cheese – with salad, followed by a coffee and a chocolate orange. Then I have another one in the afternoon, or sometimes two…"

"Sandwiches or cups of coffee?"

"I'm sorry?"

"You have another one or two sandwiches in the afternoon?"

"No, chocolate oranges."

"Segments?"

I stare blankly at the doctor.

"You have another one or two segments of a…"

"Chocolate orange. No, whole ones. One small piece leads to another and before you realise, you've eaten the whole thing, you know how it is…" The doctor raises her eyebrows and types something into her computer.

"Have you ever had one? I've got one if you'd like to try a bit?" I reach into my bag and pull out a foil wrapped piece of chocolate. The doctor shakes her head and I wonder if she'd notice if I popped a piece in my mouth.

"Please continue, I think we are up to your evening meal."

"Dinner is usually bangers and mash or spag bol – all home cooked," I continue, "except for on Friday when we treat ourselves to a takeaway curry."

"And that's a full day's eating?" the doctor asks. "A little fruit for dessert perhaps?"

I shake my head, "Maybe a chocolate orange."

"And that's it then for the day?"

"Well, I sometimes have a last one with my tea before bed."

"A last what?"

"Chocolate orange."

67

The doctor turns and addresses me with a steady gaze, "And what do you drink apart from tea and coffee?"

"Water mainly, I get very thirsty."

"Water is good, it hydrates the body," she says and I relax a bit in my chair. Maybe it's not so bad after all. Lots of people enjoy the occasional treat don't they?

"It's probably all that chocolate that is making you thirsty but it must also be having an impact on your blood sugar and by eating so much of it, there is a risk of diabetes. You will need to have a blood test." I flinch at this last part; anything that involves a needle always makes me feel a bit queasy.

"And what about alcohol?"

"Never touch the stuff," I lie, remembering when I passed out at the office Christmas party.

"Your basic diet doesn't sound too bad," the doctor continues, "but you need to drastically cut down on all that sweet stuff. It sounds like you have become addicted to chocolate."

"Chocolate orange," I correct her. "Not just any chocolate."

The doctor stares at me for a moment and I can feel myself blushing. "I don't eat any other sweets," I say by way of explanation. "But chocolate orange well, it just tastes so good."

"What about exercise?"

"Well," I think for a moment, clutching for something positive to say. "I walk every day."

"Walking is good for you. How far would you say?"

"Um, to the shop and back, about half a mile." I neglect to mention the all too frequent occasions when I have cleaned out supplies of chocolate orange from our nearest shop and I drive the two miles to the supermarket.

"Do you take any other form of exercise?"

"Well, I was thinking of joining a gym but the last time I injured myself…"

"Always remember to warm up before attempting any exercise to reduce the risk of injury," the doctor interrupts again, a little rudely I think.

"… lifting my bag up into the locker."

The doctor sighs. "And how are you sleeping?"

"Not well but then that's not really surprising with all the tossing and turning at night. It's not easy you see," I pat my growing tummy, "with the baby almost due."

"Have you tried using a pillow?"

I look down at my huge stomach, "I don't think I really need one."

"To support the bump at night, it can help in finding a comfortable position to sleep."

"Pillows, cushions, the bed has more peaks than Mount Everest."

The doctor throws me a last exasperated look and I can sense my imminent dismissal. "I think then, it's simply a case of reducing the amount of chocolate you eat. I suggest cutting down gradually to reduce the symptoms of withdrawal," she says, handing me a form for my blood test.

"But surely it's not that big a deal. Unusual cravings are common during pregnancy and at least it's not coal or some other weird stuff like that. Our neighbour used to send her poor old husband out at all hours to buy Coal Tar soap – imagine that!"

The doctor gets up and opens the door. "Pregnant women, yes, Mr Johnston, but not their husbands. Please send my regards to your wife and be sure to let me know as soon as the baby arrives. Maybe then you will both begin to feel better – and lose some of that 'baby' weight!"

Something

By Trisha Todd

I want to find something I'm good at,
Something I do really well.
I want to find something I'm good at,
Something in which I excel.
I don't know the thing that will grab me,
The interest that my mind will hold
But I do hope I find what this thing is,
Before I get just too damn old!

Mediterranean

By Josephine Gibson

She sat out on the decking, legs stretched, sandals kicked off, her feet rubbing the grooves of the wood beneath her. For a moment she closed her eyes and turned her face upwards, enjoying the sun against her skin.

At her side sat a cool glass of wine, the Chablis so cold she could draw lines with the condensation droplets. She twirled the stem of the glass between her fingers as she began to take in the view.

It was stunning. The sea was so blue today it was iridescent, the constant movement of the waves catching the light like the prisms of a diamond. The children playing in front of her were silhouettes, puppet-like they darted from bucket to sea with their nets. They squealed with delight as they found treasures; tiny little crabs rolling in the sand as the waves withdrew, flat stones their fathers sent skimming through the water, empty but undamaged sea snail shells.

She indulged herself for a moment – would life be different if she had her own children? Would she be paddling in the shallows, pointing out new discoveries, holding a fat, warm, trusting, little hand? Mother to a sweet toddler, wearing a frilly, polka dot bikini? She smiled to herself as she watched her husband approach, already sipping his litre glass of lager so it wouldn't spill.

"Hello darling," she said as she held out her cheek for a kiss. "You found me alright then."

"Phew, yes, after I'd fought my way through the crowds."

"It's such a beautiful day, everyone's out."

He nodded, crossing his ankles, sitting back in his chair and looking around. He was dressed for the beach; shorts, T-shirt, straw trilby and sunnies. A masculine sheen of sweat over the stubble on his lower jaw made her feel languidly aroused and wondering whether it might have been better to suggest a siesta rather than a walk to the beachfront cafe.

She flung her arms upwards in a stretch and said, on impulse:

"You know, I've been wondering if it's time to start a family."

He swivelled his head slowly towards her but she couldn't read the expression in his eyes which were hidden behind his sunglasses.

"What's made you say that?" he asked incredulously.

"Well, it's just sitting here, watching the children. I know I've always been a career woman – and I love the lifestyle and what it gives us" – she waved her hand to indicate the panorama before them – "but wouldn't it be great to be able to share it with a little one, to show them the beach, to teach them to swim, oh, I don't know, get them to jump over the waves and then cuddle them warm when they're so cold from the water they're shaking?"

He didn't say anything and because she felt embarrassed by the sense of longing the picture she'd drawn had created, she lowered her voice playfully and said:

"Let me have your babies."

He laughed and leaned forward, engaging her in a kiss that made her decide she'd definitely made a mistake in not suggesting a siesta. His lips were cool from the lager, and slightly bitter, his tongue probing and reminding her of afternoons lying naked in their room in the warmth of the sun. He drew back slightly, paused as though he was looking at her, then holding her chin, kissed her gently on the lips.

She knew then that something had changed, irrevocably, that a decision had been made; that a moment of madness in the sunshine was going to alter her life forever. She sighed as she looked at him: masculine but deeply human and vulnerable, and that was what made him so damn sexy.

"What?" he asked, with a sloppy, one-sided grin.

"You," she said. "You – grr! I thought I had life all sorted. You just want me chained to a kitchen sink!"

He raised an eyebrow.

"Well, if you'd like to try that..."

They both laughed then and clasped hands, knowing they'd head home when they finished their drinks.

She raised her glass and looked through to the distorted beach.

Southend-on-Sea! On a day like this you could almost believe you were in the Med.

The Incomparable Miss Cable

By Karen Richardson

Miss Cable was in her early 60s in 1975 and was an established pillar of my junior school, the church affiliated to the school and in the immediate community where she lived.

Miss Cable, (her Christian name was Norah; a fact we children whispered and laughed about when she wasn't within earshot), was about 5ft 6in with white, short, wavy hair. She was slightly plump, which gave her a softly rounded face and she had an abundance of wrinkles. Miss Cable was gimlet-eyed and was very strict as a teacher. She brooked no nonsense, at any time, and never smiled or laughed.

Norah Cable had no 'favourites' in her class and had an individual style of teaching. In the pre-Ofsted monitored days of the 1970s, she taught all of the subjects from a staunchly religious standpoint. A frequent activity to fill any spare minutes before the home time bell was for the class to find the hymn number, or title, she called out as quickly as possible in their hymn books. Miss Cable always told us in an imperious voice that: "Good, Christian children should never be idle and without occupation."

Her final task of every school day was for her to lead the class 'a capella' in singing the last four lines of

77

'Taps', to reinforce for her seven year olds that 'God is nigh'.

Miss Cable was an anachronism and quaintly old-fashioned. Her clothes, manners and mannerisms were archaic to her lively class. She wore homemade, round-necked, knee length dresses which always had a three quarter length sleeve. The material that the dresses were made from only varied slightly in colour. They were generally a blue, brown or green paisley with a silver thread pre-woven into the pattern. Every day, she had a freshly ironed, flowery handkerchief slotted into the elasticated bracelet of her wristwatch. She carried a plain navy blue handbag with a gold centre clasp and wore mid-height court shoes which matched the handbag. Miss Cable wore old-fashioned pale blue directoire knickers, which finished only an inch or so above the hem of her dress. Although she was impeccably ladylike, when she sat down, her dress hem would rise slightly and her knickers would appear for all to see. It was a source of amusement to us and a constant vexation for her, so she taught the majority of our lessons standing up by the blackboard.

Miss Cable never wore anything as frivolous as make-up. She always had an overpowering smell of herbal embrocation, which smelt stronger in the winter months, and probably meant that she was suffering from arthritis or rheumatism.

Her clothes only slightly differed on a Wednesday morning when, solemnly at 9.15am, she would put on a long sleeved, fitted jacket made of the same material as that day's dress, pull on a pair of spotless white gloves and place a plain navy hat on her head. Without looking in a mirror, she would secure the hat with a pearl hat pin. Miss Cable would then lead us, in single file and absolute silence, to our assembly in church. Once we were in our class pew, she would curtsey deeply towards the central stained glass window with a crucifixion scene depicted on it. She would then make the sign of the cross over her ample bosom and finally, would she take her place in our pew and the assembly would begin.

On our return to school for lessons, the jacket was carefully placed on a wooden hanger, the hat and hat pin into a handmade cloth bag and put into a small storage cupboard, which was locked by her until the following Wednesday. The still pristine white gloves went into her handbag inside a smaller handmade cloth bag. This was the only time during the week that she ever opened her handbag in the classroom.

Miss Cable drilled into us that we should stand up behind our desk whenever she walked into or out of the classroom. One of the boys would be nominated in advance every day to open and close the classroom door for her. They would be chosen with her command of *'Master Duggan. Would you be so kind?'* Girls were selected for more feminine tasks, such as changing the water in the small vase on Miss Cable's desk, which had one flower in every week.

I was given the dubious privilege of holding a huge, black umbrella over Miss Cable's head during our school sports day. It was during the heat wave summer of 1976 and Miss Cable called me over with, *'Miss Green. Would you oblige me please?'*

Norah Cable was the local Brownie leader and had run the group for decades. It was a special concession permitted by her, that the girls who were members of the Brownie group could wear their Brownie uniform in school on Wednesday, as the group was held immediately after school ended.

Miss Cable organised and ran her Brownie group in the same way as she taught inside school; very structured with educational pursuits and games. Religious material would be included in any activity that she possibly could. We invariably learnt semaphore, simple first aid or how to polish our shoes. Miss Cable would only countenance very quiet games such as 'Pin the Bobble Hat on the Brownie' or sedate 'Charades,' acting out book titles.

Miss Cable wasn't an inspirational teacher. In fact, I'm not even sure that she liked children very much. She was however a strong-minded woman who I will always remember with affection.

If the Wind Should Blow

By Debbie Softly

My daughter small and precious
I loved to watch her play
If the wind should blow around her
Then gently I would say,
"It's chilly now, the sun has gone
Come... put your jumper on."

Her teenage clothes were skimpy
Her attitude was bold
If the wind should blow around her
I feared she'd feel the cold;
"It's chilly now, the sun has gone
Come... put your jumper on."

Next she became a mother
Emotions were a whirl
If the wind should blow around her
She'd whisper to her girl,
"It's chilly now, the sun has gone
Come... put your jumper on."

My daughter watches me now
Dozing quietly in my chair
If the wind should blow around me

I sleep on, unaware;
"It's chilly now, the sun has gone
Mum... put your jumper on."

Auld Fruity

By Barbara Sleap

Judy let her mother in; they greeted each other with a warm hug and entered the kitchen where Judy had laid out the ingredients and utensils that they were going to need. Judy's mum was about to share the secret of 'Auld Fruity' with her. 'Auld Fruity' was a cake made to a recipe handed down from Judy's Scottish grandmother and was no ordinary fruit cake; her mother made it for family celebrations and events and would share the recipe with no one. But today she was going to share the secret with Judy.

"It's time for you to learn the recipe, Jude," said her mum, handing Judy a yellowed piece of paper with neat writing on it. Judy looked at her mother. She was worried about her; Judy's dad had died suddenly over a year ago and her mum had lost her sparkle since his death. Their little terraced house wasn't the same without his vibrant presence and although her mum had plenty of friends and visitors she just seemed to be going through the motions. She had also suffered various minor illnesses and was always visiting the doctor, something she never did before.

"Right, let's make a start," her mum said enthusiastically and set to, creaming butter and sugar while Judy prepared a cake tin, cracked eggs and measured fruit, nuts and spices. They chatted while they worked and Judy giggled as her mum described the last WI meeting she had been to.

Judy watched her mother thoughtfully. It was strange really, she had eaten this cake many times but had never seen her mother, or indeed her grandmother, make it. It was baked for Judy's wedding; her mother and grandmother had made one each and had them professionally iced for the occasion. The cake was always the focal point on the table at Christmas and there was rarely any left over by Boxing Day. There was even one at her father's funeral. He had loved to cut it and serve everyone, keeping a large slice for himself while jokingly saying he had made it.

Her mother was now fully engrossed in the task, stirring the mixture carefully.

"You must add the eggs with a metal spoon," she said as Judy reached for her hand mixer. "There is no easy way with this recipe."

The final task was to add some whiskey. Judy poured out a small glass each and they toasted each other with a smile. "Here's to Auld Fruity."

At last the mixture was finished and Judy carefully and lovingly poured it into the prepared tin. She set the timer on the oven and made some tea while they waited for it to cook.

****

Brr... brr... Judy woke with a start and turned off the alarm, trying to gather her thoughts. Her dream had seemed so real, almost as if her mum had been there. Judy could even smell the aroma of baking as she headed for the shower. Thoughts of her mum came rushing back. She had died three months earlier, quietly and sadly; the family had been devastated.

Judy wished her husband John was here and not working in the States. He was due home tomorrow, as were the twins James and Dan who were on a school trip. She had missed them all, and had especially missed her mum popping in for coffee and a chat. Perhaps she would have a go at making the cake for their homecoming. Yes, that's what she would do. She had found the yellowed paper recipe whilst clearing her mum's things. It would probably be a bit hit and miss, but in time Judy was sure she could perfect it and keep the tradition alive.

Judy pottered around in the bedroom for a while but was unable to shake off the dream and the vivid thoughts of her mum, she still smelt the aroma of baking around the house. She gathered up some laundry and went downstairs. On entering the kitchen the smell was unmistakable; Judy dropped her clothes and gasped in amazement, as there on the table, on one of her mum's favourite plates, with two small slices already neatly cut, was 'Auld Fruity'.

Domestic Bliss?

By Trisha Todd

"Ow! God that hurt," John shouted to Fiona, who was washing up in the kitchen.

"What have you done now?" she called.

"That pesky cat, scratched me again. I don't know what's got into it. Look, cuts all over. How can something so small hurt so much? Like paper cuts – sting out of all proportion."

"Well leave the cat alone; he doesn't like you teasing him – you never know when to stop." Fiona put the last of the dishes away and peered at the windows. Wondering how they got dirty so quickly, she reached for the window cleaner and gave them a going over.

"I'm bleeding too. I can't believe it!" John continued.

"I'm sure it will stop hurting soon," she soothed and carried on with her work. *Those windows won't clean themselves you know.*

"Aargh! I can't fold this newspaper now either, cos it hurts across my knuckles. Flipping cat!" Amid much rustling, the cat gave a sharp wail. Fiona sighed and started cleaning the floor.

"Babe, can you make a cuppa while you are out there?" John whined. "I *would* do it but my hands still hurt."

"Yes, okay. Just a minute," she replied, resting the mop against the wall and reaching for the kettle.

"My fingers are going numb – do you think he caught a nerve? Should I have a tetanus?" he panicked.

"No, I'm sure they'll be fine, stop worrying! Look, have your cup of tea and I'll bring you some biscuits."

"Ah, thanks darlin'. What would I do without you?" he smiled, as Fiona made her way awkwardly into the room, carrying the tray one-handed. "At least that cat didn't trip me up like you; it'd be tricky if I'd broken my leg as well!"

Night Night

By Kim Kimber

"Night night," I pull the duvet up to my son's chin and kiss the top of his head. "Sleep tight." He closes his eyes and I sit on the bed and stroke his hair in an effort to soothe away some of his hurt, to prevent bad thoughts from crowding his mind.

His eyes flicker open. Vivid blue eyes like those of his mother, Jodie. With the blond hair that frames his face, it is like looking at a miniature version of her. My chest tightens and I struggle to catch my breath.

"You forgot to say, 'don't let the bedbugs bite'," Luke says accusingly. I stare at him in confusion. "It's the next line. You didn't say it."

"I forgot, sorry Luke."

"I can't sleep unless you say it."

"Night night, sleep tight, don't let the bedbugs bite," I recite. It is an important part of his night-time ritual. I should have remembered, but then I'm having to learn a lot of things these days, like the fact that Luke has milk, not juice, at breakfast time and that he doesn't like cheese sandwiches in his packed lunch but cheese on toast for supper is 'awesome'.

"Mummy always used to say it, she never forgot."

"I know but mummy's not here Luke," I say gently.

"I want her back."

He starts to sob and I lift him out of bed and clutch him tightly, as if by doing so I can absorb his pain. Six years of age is too young to have your innocence stolen by illness and death. It is too soon to lose your mother.

"I miss her too Luke," I say gently, rocking him in my arms. We stay like that for a long while until he is finally overcome by fatigue and begins to snore softly in my arms. My shirt is wet with his tears as I tuck him in. Even though he is asleep, this time I don't forget. "Night night, sleep tight, don't let the bedbugs bite," I say softly.

I know that he will not rest for long; that the bad dreams will return to torment him. The ones that start out happily with him and Jodie playing outside in the sunshine, snapshots of a time now past, but the happy images quickly flicker and fade like the dying sun as the outline around his mother grows less distinct and she drifts away out of reach. He runs towards her but there is only shadow and air, no substance to hold on to and he is left alone and crying, a frightened little boy without his mother.

Luke describes his dreams to me in detail and the hardest thing to bear is that I am powerless to comfort him. As his father, the provider, I am meant to be strong, to slay dragons, to protect him but there are no weapons to fight the monsters in his mind. And when my son wakes screaming in the night, there is no medicine I can administer that will heal the hurt of losing his beloved mother. Words are useless in the face of such raw pain.

I am inert, redundant, useless, immobilised by my own grief. Jodie was my childhood sweetheart. My first and only love. Intelligent, beautiful and spirited, she lit up the lives of those around but her own light was destined to burn out too soon and I could only watch helplessly as her body was ravaged by the disease that finally claimed her. Cancer. Luke is too young to know such a word but it is forever etched upon his lips, a word he will never forget, far more damaging to his young mind than any profanity.

I go downstairs and pour myself a large whisky. Slumped in an armchair, I stare with unseeing eyes at the TV for several hours until the flickering images begin to blur and my head throbs. I pour another drink and retire for the night, lying fully clothed on my bed, trying to blot out the picture of a young Jodie, free of illness, smiling by my side.

She would berate me, I know, for giving up. "Think of Luke," I can almost hear her chide, "think of our son." I wish it had been me that had died, it should have been me. A boy needs his mother, to help him get ready for school, to watch him play and grow, to tuck him up in bed at night and hold him close when he is afraid.

I am aware of my inadequacies. My son needs me but I am not equipped to help him, paralysed by my own grief of a life without my wife and soul mate. Father and son, we both need Jodie. I can see her clearly in my mind, alive and fit, running along the beach in the sunshine, laughing, clasping a kite string, her long fair hair trailing behind her in the wind.

Suddenly, Jodie stumbles and her blue eyes look up at me in confusion, a question on her lips that can never be answered. I help her up, but she has become too weak and cannot walk unaided. I carry her and she is weightless in my arms, growing lighter by the second. By the time we reach the shade, there is nothing left but fine dust that runs through my fingers falling indistinct upon the sand, lost forever.

"Daddy, daddy, wake up." Small hands tug at my clothes, dragging me back to the present.

"What? What is it? Did you have another bad dream?"

"You were shouting." Luke scrambles up onto the bed beside me, he smells comfortingly of bed and shampoo as he wraps himself around me like a blanket. My heart is pounding and my palms are sweaty and I realise that it is I, not Luke, who has had a nightmare. And then it all comes rushing back, like watching a film on fast forward, and I can no longer hold back the tears as I remember.

Jodie before she was ill, her bravery when first diagnosed, the inner strength she found whilst undergoing chemotherapy and her refusal to give up. I remember her determination that Luke would not be affected and the fact that, until the very end, no matter how sick or weak she felt, she always had time for our son. What would she say if she could see me now?

Luke's slight frame remains steadfast. Thin arms cling on tightly while I unleash the torrent of pent up anger and emotion that I have resolutely refused to let go of since the funeral. And it is Luke who is the strong one, he holds me as if it is he who is the parent and I am a small boy, shivering, uncertain and confused. It is my son who shows me the way.

Time passes and gradually my sobs subside, my body stops shaking and I am aware of nothing except for the small boy snuggling into my side. I am spent, exhausted but the outpouring of grief has been cathartic and I reach out to Luke and draw him into a hug.

"I'm sorry Daddy," Luke says.

"Whatever for?"

"For telling you off – because you forgot the next line. I made you sad."

"You never make me sad, Luke. Daddy had a bad dream that's all."

"Like the ones I have?"

"Yes, exactly the same. It's because we both miss mummy but we'll be alright Luke, I promise, you and I. We'll get through this together."

I know it won't be easy. We have lived together as a family in the same house for every one of Luke's six years and although I thought I knew my son, I realise now that I am only just beginning to learn. It was Jodie who cared for him, who soothed cut knees, read to him, shared his successes and encouraged him to try again when he failed. Even at the end, it was Jodie who held things together, organising our lives from her sickbed so that we didn't have to worry about the mundane detail of life.

"Daddy," Luke hesitates, suddenly unsure of himself now that our roles have reverted back to father and son. "Can I sleep here tonight?" It is not something that would have happened when Jodie was alive. She would have carried Luke back to his bed and stroked his forehead until he slept, leaving me slumbering unaware.

"Of course you can Luke," I say wrapping the duvet around him. "Night night, sleep tight, don't let the bedbugs bite," I recite unprompted, but he is already dozing.

It is time to move on. I can no longer allow myself to be suffocated by despair; there is someone other than me to think of. Nothing will bring Jodie back but she will always be with us, in our hearts and memories, and she will live on in the small boy slumbering peacefully beside me.

One Size Fits All

By Karen Richardson

Scene in a wedding shop

"Can I help you?"

"Well, I'm not too sure what I'm after really. The style, I mean."

"I'm certain I'll be able to find the exact look for your special day."

"Can you give me an idea of your price range please? My budget is fairly limited, I'm afraid."

"Most customers who shop at La Belle Époque choose their perfect, dream dress first and then simply glance at the price tag as an afterthought. Nothing is as important as your big day and the cost is immaterial. La Belle Époque has a full range of all the leading designers. Walk this way please."

"I'm still not sure if this is right for me. I think..."

"Oh, I insist. At La Belle Époque we can find something for everyone. Will your bridesmaids and the lucky mother of the bride be joining us today? I have a beautiful dress suit in eau de Nil which I imagine would flatter your mother, assuming you look like her. The matching eau de Nil hat has a double layer, chin length veil and the dress suit is styled to cover up and hide all of her lumps and bumps. Talking of bumps, when is your baby due?"

"I, I don't need..."

"It's easier for us at La Belle Époque if we are aware of all the circumstances concerning your happy day in order for us to provide a complete service."

"You've made a mistake. I'm not pregn..."

"Can you imagine yourself in this stunning satin and tulle creation? The stacking of the bustle design at the back will detract from all your problem areas and you can carry a big bouquet. I think it will possibly need to be a very wide and long bouquet too. That will minimise your visual impact when you enter the church. That would only be an improvement, I think."

"I was actually hoping for..."

"Yes, this satin will deflect the oily sheen of your skin. Have you considered booking a late afternoon, winter wedding? Possibly a candlelight service?"

"I don't think you understand. You really don't have anything here that I need. I think I'll come back another day thank you."

"We pride ourselves at La Belle Époque on not letting any bride-to-be leave this establishment without selling her our full package. I think you should try on this dress. It's the only one in the shop fitted with an extra-strength whalebone corset. I'm certain if the material doesn't meet across your broad back and fasten up, that we have an embellished woollen poncho that you could wear to cover the tight fit. Yes, yes, and that poncho has a very deep hood which will help to cover your protruding ears. A poncho will be perfect for your winter wedding!"

"No, but my wedding is on the beach in Cyprus. On 15 June. Please, I just..."

"Now, for your wedding shoes. My goodness. What size are your feet? They're enormous!"

"Erm. Size nine."

"We carry a very limited range in that size. Here they are. Plain, flat and with sturdy Velcro fastenings. Well, they will be hidden by the enveloping fabric of the dress, I suppose."

"I really would like to leave..."

"So that's the dress, shoes and poncho finalised. I'll put a veil in the box too. I know you haven't tried it on but believe me, I know it is just what you need. This veil is triple milled Nottingham lace and I think you'll find it very flattering as well as helping to disguise your facial stubble. Have you considered heavy duty laser treatment on that? I have a cousin who is halfway through a six week course in acupuncture, 3D laser, Botox and teeth whitening. I have a card here with her contact details. Give her a call and mention my name and I know she will be..."

"I can't believe this! I am only trying to get next door into the men's suit hire department."

"Oh! Are you a man? Really? Pity. Still, take my cousin's business card. Perhaps she can help with your yellow teeth, but I can't promise. Anyway, do send your mother in to see us. That eau de Nil hat and dress suit has been in our stockroom for far too long. Or, it might even be suitable for your fiancée. Good morning."

The prospective groom leaves as quickly as possible.

Sky Line

By Josephine Gibson

The sky stretched ahead of her.

She remembered her husband saying that good photos were divided into thirds, and standing here she felt that she was captured in a moment of time: caught between a third of earth, a third of sea, and a third of blue, blue sky. A warm wind blew gently around her, and beneath her feet she could feel the stubble of August straw.

It was not possible to hear the sea; it lay too far beneath her. Instead she could look out across a vast, rippled tablecloth of water that shone in the sunlight. Not for her to imagine the force of the tide, rushing in, spilling over, crashing into caverns and being beaten back by cold, black, barnacle covered rock. No, she didn't want to think about that.

Instead she gazed towards the horizon, enjoying the peace, the illusion of calm, the snapshot, the fragment of time that spoke of softness, seductively whispering that all was well.

A seagull wheeled overhead, its cry cutting through the moment. She became aware of the sun on her neck, a slight, prickling sensation that told her she was beginning to burn. She felt that the wind was picking up and she clutched at the sides of her cardigan. She hadn't realised how close to the cliff edge she had stood, and could not say how long she had been standing there. It was late, she needed to get back, there would be people waiting.

As she turned the sun continued to shine, dazzling white with no defined edges. She had to shade her eyes to see her way home.

I Spy

By Sandra Casey

I stood in the doorway looking at the faces that passed me by. I wondered whether I would still recognise her. I haven't seen her for 24 years. I look down at my wrist to see the time but curse myself and remember my watch is sitting on the side in the bathroom. I look around for a clock in the street. I don't want to speak to anyone.

Why has this happened?

Why am I anxious?

I concentrate on my breathing and count to three, hold for three, blow out for three. And feel sick. So I stop. There's a church at the end of the street and I look up to see if it has a clock. Two fifteen. No, it can't be 2:15. I left at nine and it should have only taken me 20 minutes to walk here. Bloody hell!

Why did she ring?

"It's life or death." That's what she said. "It's a life or death situation, Cath. I need you to meet me. You're the only one I can trust."

What!!???

"I don't bloody know you Brigitte! We haven't seen each other in years. YEARS!"

"Look I can't explain now but I need you to go to the Moroccan door at East Street for 10 o'clock. Wait for me. Even if I'm late. If I'm not there by 11, then go. And don't call me. Just forget I rang."

"But…" And the line was dead.

I didn't have her number so I couldn't ring back. My irritation turned to annoyance and then rage. Why had she rung ME of all people?

I had walked into the kitchen and poured myself a large wine, kicked the bin and shouted "Sh-h-iiit!!!" at the top of my lungs! Walking back into the lounge I had slumped down on the sofa and relived the call. But there wasn't much to remember. It was only brief and it said nothing.

And everything.

Brigitte was a fighter. A survivor. She didn't need anyone. We met at university and made friends within hours of meeting each other. We had different friends and mixed in different circles but we were drawn together like magnets when things didn't go well. She had rung me because she knew I wouldn't ask too many questions, because she knew I wouldn't crumble at the sign of danger, that I would know she needed me, and that I was a fighter and survivor too.

'Life or death situation'.

The words rang in my head like church bells on a Sunday morning. It was loud and jumbled. I couldn't make sense of it. I could hear the words 'life and death' but no explanation to go with them while they pounded in my head. I had no understanding of what might come next. I couldn't think straight standing here. Suddenly I felt exposed. I looked out for a better place. Across the walkway was a small park with dense Victorian planting, a row of yew trees and a couple of benches.

I ran. Not waiting to think again. My instinct told me my first decision was a good one. Now in the park I quickly walked to a good view where I could see the whole street. I stood at the side of a tree and took out a cigarette. I focused on looking relaxed and waited.

My mind took me back 24 years. I had a vision of Brigitte. Such passion and drive. Dangerous and exciting. She had been chosen early. Plucked from all of us other students for her intelligence and ability. I had not been surprised. She had never said what she did, but in my heart I knew that she was a dream candidate for being a spy.

"Cath!" I swivelled round nearly falling. She stood looking at me slightly hesitant as to whether she should hug me or not. "I'm sorry but I couldn't think of who else to call. I'm in danger," she said.

"From who?" I said. She looked at me like she wanted to tell me everything but thought better of it and said, "I've been on the run for a while... there's a double agent. You know I'm a spy so I don't need to explain but I need a place to hide. You're the only person I can trust and they won't find me with you. We've no connections anymore."

I let out a deep breath and sighed. I looked down and my shoelace was undone. I bent down to do it up. Standing up slowly, I stared into her eyes and watched her expression change from urgency to confusion and then terror as I raised the gun and shot her through the heart.

And for just one moment, remembered, I had loved her.

Running Wild

By Debbie Softly

No one can reach her
nothing is clear
so she turns up the music
the melody masks her fear.
She piles on the make-up
and wears her sexy dress
there's nothing to show
her emotions are a mess.
So,
She screams like a baby
tantrums like a child
life is in turmoil
young woman running wild.

She aches to go forward
but something holds her back
she doesn't understand
how to keep on track.
It's all within her grasp
yet so far out of reach
she tries to break away
still clinging like a leech.

So,
She screams like a baby
tantrums like a child
life is in turmoil
young woman running wild.

Nothing seems to hurt her
does she really care?
Life is for living
cross her if you dare
everybody's party girl
she fills her life with fun
is it only me that sees
how she wants to run?
When
She screams like a baby
tantrums like a child
life is in turmoil
young woman running wild.

Happy Harry

By Karen Richardson

The Reverend George Wood was such a well-known character around the Southchurch seafront area before the First World War that for over 50 years he was commemorated by a plaque, which has now unfortunately been removed.

From looking at photographs and speaking to people who saw him preach in his later years, he was a sturdily built man, always dressed in a dog collar and with a ready smile.

Day-trippers and locals alike referred to him as 'Happy Harry' because of the evangelical style of the hymns he exhorted passers-by to join in with, such as 'It's rolling in, it's rolling in, the sea of love, is rolling in'. Happy Harry would provide the accompaniment for his fluid congregation from a small harmonium that he carried down to the seafront on his back. He sat next to a sign that he erected beside him which informed everyone that he was 'Happy Harry, Southend's Unsupported Evangelist'.

Happy Harry would also preach a 'hell and brimstone' sermon, which generally had to be shouted, due to the level of abuse and heckling directed at him, in addition to the volume of noise normally associated with a sunny, busy weekend at the seafront. In its heyday,

Southend attracted thousands of day-trippers who considered Happy Harry fair prey and an intrinsic part of their day's entertainment.

Happy Harry would take a collection both during and after his open air service by encouraging the congregated day-trippers to 'give us an'apenny jus fer Jesus'. A proportion of the more drunken ones would throw sharpened coins at him or wrap a low value coin inside silver paper to make their donation to the collection look more sizeable than it actually was. When he had had enough of the tirade, he would load his harmonium on his back, gather up all of the coins and retreat to the Falcon pub for a restorative drink or two.

The *Southend Standard* in the early 1930s frequently carried small articles about Happy Harry having offensive notes pinned onto his jacket or of being physically jostled, and a passing policeman having to intervene to 'save' him.

It could be thought that Happy Harry had the ultimate last laugh though. A mix of rumours and local records say that after his retirement, Happy Harry drove a large expensive car and owned a string of properties across the South East area. He spent his final years in a comfortable retirement home in South London and died in 1974, aged 86-years-old.

Other rumours query whether he was actually ordained and how much, if any, of those seafront collections found their way to the church at all.

Voyeur

By Kim Kimber

She is easy to spot. There is something about her body
language that marks her out from the other people on the
beach; nervous and excitable, not carefree and relaxed
like other passers-by. She looks out of place somehow
amongst the casual dog walkers, early morning runners
and pensioners sat on benches reading their newspapers.
Smartly dressed in a figure-hugging navy skirt and snug-
fitting white blouse, she looks as if she would be more at
home behind a desk than at the seaside. Her clothes are
just that bit too tight, the heels of her shoes a little too
high for her to be taken seriously in the boardroom.
More decorative than decision-making, I decide
unkindly.

The girl's hair, which I imagine to be long and wild
when loose, is piled high on her head and from this
distance it looks as if it is a fashionable fiery red; but I
am too far away to tell if it is natural. I cannot see her
face but she appears somewhat elfin-like and fragile-
looking and I imagine her with pointed features and pale
skin. I wish that I could see her eyes and I wonder if
they are blue, or green like a cat's. I believe that you can
tell a lot about a person by their eyes such as if they are
kind or cruel, honest or deceitful.

It is a beautiful morning, already warm in spite of the early hour, and she carries her jacket. The tide is out but the air is thick with ozone and the promise of a full, fat, lazy stretch of ocean just over the horizon, ready to gorge itself once more on the waiting sand. Seagulls dip and swoop overhead seeking out tasty morsels on the land below, diving as they hunt for potential snacks of chips and bread abandoned by careless tourists. How I envy those birds their freedom and the ability to fly away on the beat of a wing.

Removing her impractical shoes, she hops about barefoot, as if her feet are connecting with hot Mediterranean sand in the midday sun and not the cool, damp variety of the English coastline. She is killing time, waiting for someone. I wonder when he will show up.

I see him before she does, striding along the beach towards her, confident, arrogant and self-assured. He too is smartly dressed. He wears a well-cut, bespoke suit and moves with the bearing of someone who is used to getting his own way. Even at this distance, I can imagine his smell; clean, with a hint of expensive pine cologne reeking of power and masculinity.

The girl is ridiculously young compared to me, no more than 18 or 19, and I run my hand over my face, tracing each wrinkle with the tip of my finger. *Curse her,* I mutter to myself, *for her youth and vitality.* He is much older than her although he moves with agility and there is a jauntiness to his step. I can't see his face but I know that he has strong features and a receding hairline. He is vain, and works out at the gym, maybe so that he can keep pace with his young girlfriend.

Spotting him coming towards her, she skips along the sand, and leaps cat-like into his embrace. He swings her round as easily as if she were weightless, a mere child in his arms. She stumbles slightly as he sets her back down on the sand and she hangs on to him for support, her head resting against his chest. I imagine the rhythmic beat of his heart, racing slightly in anticipation, the slight hint of his chest hair beneath his shirt.

She lifts her head expectantly and he looks around quickly before dipping his head to kiss her. It lasts for only the briefest of seconds, barely more than a brush of the lips, but in that moment I taste his mouth, breathe in his scent and feel his desire.

I sense that they haven't been lovers for long. Their movements are furtive and explorative, lacking the fluidity and ease of more familiar couples. Each is still largely a mystery to the other, and they are not yet weighed down by the expectation, responsibility and commitment of a long-term relationship.

From my clifftop position I am unable to hear what they are saying as they whisper to one another but I watch as he laughs at something she says, and I wonder if he really finds it funny or if he is merely playing with her. Is he toying with her as a cat does a captured mouse, savouring the satisfaction of having trapped its prey?

111

They walk away from the scene, hand in hand, and I imagine how safe she must feel with her fingers entwined with his, naively thinking that she is 'the one', or that she might be able to tame him, believing that he will never let go. He looks down at her and I picture his smile and the dimple on his chin.

A woman approaches and they quickly break apart, like teenagers caught kissing by a disapproving parent. He nods to the woman and she passes by without looking back but they continue to walk separately. No longer physically connected, they are joined by the crackle of electricity, the powerful force that is their desire for one another. They are almost out of sight but in my mind's eye, I can make out their footsteps side by side in the sand as they walk away.

The two of them are safe – for now – or so they believe. They assume that their secret remains undiscovered and that no one has seen them, but if they had paused for a moment to look up, they might have caught a glimpse of a lonely figure on the clifftop and the woman who is watching them.

Me – his wife!

The Appointment

By Trisha Todd

"Come on, Bobby. It's time for your appointment."

Sue shrugged her coat over her shoulders and retrieved the car keys from a pocket. Then she waited. And waited.

"Bobby!" she shouted. "We'll be late."

"Don't care. Don't want to go." The response drifted down the stairs, accompanied by the sound of stamping.

"Oh for goodness' sake – don't make me come up there."

Sue stood at the bottom of the stairs, as Bobby appeared, brow furrowed and eyes dark. Sue couldn't help but laugh.

"Come on, it won't be that bad, promise."

She could hear him mumbling to himself in the car, stopping only when they reached the dentist's door. Standing behind him to cut off any retreat, she ushered him into the waiting room.

"You can go through now," the receptionist advised with a smile.

Sue took Bobby's coat from him, ignoring the look in his eyes. "You don't need me in there with you – you're quite old enough to go on your own."

He turned and walked towards the dentist's door as though to his doom.

The walls of the surgery could probably have been thicker, as the whole waiting room could hear Bobby's wails and pleading, and Sue shrunk into her seat. The dentist's voice boomed out.

"It'll only take a moment, if you can open your mouth a little wider and stop moving. I'm not going to hurt you, you know."

Sue couldn't hear Bobby's response over the sniggers. She sighed and rolled her eyes at the couple sitting opposite. Less than five minutes later, Bobby emerged, happy to be leaving at last.

"That wasn't so bad," he smiled.

"I should think not!" Sue retorted, indignant. "It was only a check-up after all."

With that, she grasped her husband's hand and marched him out of the building.

Bygone Days

By Sandra Casey

As she lay in her bed
Thinking of the day ahead
She looked through her window of life
Remembering her time as a dutiful wife.

Days filled, with many good deeds
Building a family, sowing her seeds
Years of growing, creating a nest
Taking a back seat, from all the rest.

Then one day, her husband passed on
Her children grown, the bustle all gone
It's only her now, all on her own
Filling her clear day, without a moan.

And she smiles at the glory
Of her beautiful, rich story
She had a wonderful life
And she was a very good wife.

Past and Present

By Barbara Sleap

"Good morning Michael, nice to meet you again."

"Hi Pauline, how are you? Thanks for coming."

"Yes, I'm well thank you, let's go in and see Doris shall we?"

They walked along the hospital corridor and arrived at the entrance to St Margaret's Ward.

"Michael, before we go in I ought to tell you that I might be asking Doris some rather searching questions. Magnolia House is not registered for residents with Dementia or Alzheimer's, and I have to be sure."

"That's fine Pauline, not a problem, I'm pretty sure she's OK in that area."

They entered the ward and approached the bed where Doris was sitting turning the pages of a magazine. Pauline could see her disability silhouetted beneath the covers. Doris looked up coughed and smiled.

"Hello Doris, I'm Pauline, it's so good to meet you. I expect Michael's told you that he and the twins, Paul and Dan, came and visited Magnolia House last week. We look forward to welcoming you there because it's a happy little home and we have lots going on. How do you feel about giving up your flat?"

"Well, I am finding things a bit difficult, my diabetes never seems stable nowadays and my leg doesn't seem to fit anymore as I think I must have lost weight, they don't give you much to eat in here. I seem to spend a lot more time in a wheelchair, which I hate. They told me about the home though; it's near the sea isn't it?"

Michael glanced at Pauline.

"Well, not really Doris, it's nearer to London."

"Oh, that's a shame, I like the sea."

"Doris, I'd like to find out a bit more about you, could you tell me where you born?"

"Romford, 14 August 1911."

"Goodness that makes you 97 this year, you must have seen lots of changes in your life?"

"Yes, I have, I remember the good old days. The war and my house in London, all my friends. They never visit me."

"Lot of memories then!"

"Will I have my own room in this place?"

"Of course, Doris, and your own bathroom."

"What about television? I don't want to miss my soaps, I'm already behind being stuck in here."

"Your own television and whatever else you would like to bring. What are your favourite soaps then Doris?"

"Well there's *Coronation Street*, that's my real favourite, I love watching Ena Sharples in The Snug in the pub. I also like *EastEnders* and er, oh what's it called, the one about the farm. Oh, you know, er, *The Archers*, it's on every night on BBC1."

Michael frowned at his mother.

118

Pauline looked at Michael thoughtfully.

Doris coughed loudly.

"I understand you have grandchildren and great grandchildren Doris, tell me about them."

"Well, I've got three grandsons; Gary, James and Robert, two great granddaughters; Holly and Daisy, then there's Liam and Thomas too."

"You have a lot of birthdays to remember then."

"Yes, I always send cards but I never see them nowadays and do you know…"

Michael interrupted her, "Mum, Gary was here the other day with Michelle and the girls, they bought you some drawings."

"Did they, it seems ages ago."

"And Paul came yesterday with James."

Doris coughed.

"They couldn't have stayed for long then."

"They were here all afternoon, mum."

Pauline looked concerned

"Doris, have you got any questions to ask me before I go?"

"Yes, will I have my own room? And will my Bob be able to stay with me sometimes? I miss my Bob."

"Was he your husband Doris?"

Doris' eyes filled with tears and she coughed again.

Michael just stared disbelievingly.

"Mum," he faltered, "are you alright?"

"Not really Mike, I'm tired now."

She coughed again.

Pauline stood up ready to leave.

"That's a nasty cough you've got Doris."

Doris sat up straight and stared at Pauline. "Yes, well what do you expect, they left me in the park all night."

My Greenhouse

By Debbie Softly

The patio door slides with a satisfying swish; instantly the warm sun pours into the house. I stand in the doorway and let the heat slowly creep from my upturned face right down to my sandals and in between my toes. My peachy, polished toenails look almost too bright in the glaring sunlight.

Although still early, I can hear the distant hum of lawnmowers, buzzing like bees behind the fences. The familiar smell of freshly cut grass will soon overpower the heady scent of the honeysuckle. My own lawn, cut yesterday, stands proud in its neatness; the daisies lurking under the turf have yet to surface again and create their patchwork pattern amongst the greenery.

Behind me in the house, I hear the clatter of breakfast being made; the aroma of toast competes for attention through wafts of sizzling bacon. Water gushes noisily through the downpipe, as upstairs someone is showering away the night's sleepy grime.

I finish the last of my coffee, before walking into the garden. The sparkly, dewy grass softens to my tread and tickles my feet. I walk with purpose, barely glancing at the tall majestically sweeping willow tree, its branches dancing and swaying in the breeze, so focused am I on my destination.

Once there I pause for a few seconds, the metal frame, rusty with age in places, gives this ungainly structure character. It stands solidly year after year, boldly withstanding the relentless winter weather. Its roof a resting place for windswept spring blossom, and inside a blistering furnace, come the summer.

As I pull back the glass door I am greeted with the smell of damp soil from last night's watering session which, mixed with today's warmth, makes it seem almost steamy.

The young tomato plants green and healthy, as yet without fruit, cling shyly to their canes for support. I bend to inspect and prick out unwanted shoots; their tiny immature leaves feel furry in my fingers.

The rows of little brown pots which once contained small seedlings, now reward me with a carpet of leaves. All now too large for their plastic homes, each struggling and jostling for more space to grow, they patiently await my help.

The muscles in my arms begin to tense with the effort of carrying out the weighty bags of compost. I sit down on the ground but despite the warmth on my body and a slight trickle of sweat forming on my brow, my bottom begins to feel damp through my jeans.

I delve both hands into the bag, mixing and crumbling the soil with my hands, kneading and folding the mixture gently, as if I were making pastry. I smooth out unwanted lumps as I fill the tubs. Once bright smart terracotta, now faded and stained from previous years' use.

As I work, my fingers feel that familiar heaviness from the mud which has caught and stuck under my nails. Back in the house do they wonder where I am? No, they know me too well. It's late May and the sun creeps around the garden enveloping every corner with its soothing presence.

Mum is, of course, down at her greenhouse.

Elizabeth

By Kim Kimber

She is pruning her roses when I approach. Snip, snip, snip, the dead buds fly in all directions, her practised hands moving steadily across the thorny stems.

"Morning Elizabeth," I say, "have you got time for a cuppa?"

"Oh that would be lovely dear," she replies, "I'll just tidy up these things."

She gets up slowly and I watch her unfurl like a cat, her lithe body fit from years of gardening and yoga. Her natural agility belies her years. Elizabeth stretches, removes her gloves and makes her way towards the shed with the secateurs. Every movement is graceful and, as usual, I feel huge and awkward in her company.

Having put away her gardening equipment, Elizabeth closes the shed door and bolts it securely. "Now about that tea, why don't you pop into mine? I've got a lovely batch of scones, fresh out of the oven."

Of course you have, I think to myself fondly, wondering if there is anything this woman isn't good at. "Yours it is," I say with a smile, both of us knowing that all I have to offer is half a packet of stale digestives.

Elizabeth's kitchen is warm and cosy. The delicious smell of baking wafts under my nose as she thrusts a plate of still warm scones into my hand.

125

"There should be some homemade jam on the shelf. Choose what you fancy and make yourself comfortable."

Marvelling, as usual, at the neatly stacked jars and tins, the clear uncluttered surfaces and general sense of order, I scan the labels and select a jar labelled 'Strawberry 2012' written in Elizabeth's looping handwriting. I pull out a chair and sit down.

"Tea or coffee?" she asks.

"Coffee please." Seconds later she places a mug of steaming frothy liquid on the table in front of me. "Milky and sweet, just how you like it," she says. Elizabeth takes hers strong and black without sugar.

"So, how are things with you?" she asks, settling down into the chair opposite me.

"Oh, you know, much the same as usual." I shrug; Elizabeth knows me too well for me to lie. She can read my every thought and she pats my hand sympathetically.

"Teenagers again? It will get easier in time," she says wisely. "They all find their way in the end." Elizabeth should know I guess; she has had six of her own, all grown up now with lives, jobs and a brood of children of their own who all love to come and visit 'grannie Betty'.

I regard the woman across the table with affection. Her hair is short and neat. Today it is a light copper, with pale yellow highlights. Last month Elizabeth went blond and for a while before that, auburn. One time, she opened the door and her hair was brassy orange. "I don't always get it right," she had chuckled.

She wears only the slightest trace of make-up but her complexion is clear and her eyes are bright and alert. Elizabeth isn't what you would describe as beautiful, even in the photos from her younger days, but she has an openness and honesty that draws you in, that and an unmistakable mischievous sparkle in her eyes. She is small and slight, strong as an ox and rarely ill.

"So what is it this time?" she asks, "are those girls running rings around you again?"

I nod over the rim of my cup, "I never seem to know where they are, who they are with or what time they will be home, and you should see the state of their rooms."

Elizabeth chuckles, "I remember it well and in my day there were no mobile phones to keep track of them." As if on cue, Elizabeth's mobile beeps loudly, announcing the arrival of a text. She puts on her reading glasses and smiles broadly, "WI need a batch of cakes for this Saturday's fundraiser."

I spread a generous portion of jam on a scone and feel myself starting to relax.

"Might as well let them have some fun while they are young," she continues wisely, resuming our conversation, "as long as you are there to hold their hands when things don't work out, they'll always want to come back home. They will always need their mum you know."

I form a mental image of my earlier argument with the twins and wince at the memory. All of us shouting at the same time with me threatening to empty the contents of their bedroom floors into a bin bag, the girls leaving together, slamming the front door behind them, me sobbing in the hall. I doubt either of them will be keen to see their mum for quite some time.

I have never seen Elizabeth cry, although I have worked my way through several boxes of tissues in her company. Even when her cat died, she scooped up the dead animal and, refusing all help, buried her beloved pet in the garden under a rose bush without shedding one tear. "They bred them strong in my day," I have often heard her say, "I have lived through war and there is no time for sentiment when there are bombs dropping on your head. If you can survive that, you can do anything."

Elizabeth is the woman all her neighbours turn to for advice and comfort when their own lives get over-complicated and messy. "There's not much in the world that can't be fixed by tea and talking," she says often.

I take a sip of delicious coffee and vow to be calm and welcoming when the girls eventually return home, as I know they will, they are good girls really.

"Feeling a bit better now?" Elizabeth asks as I drain my cup.

I nod, feeling foolish about my earlier argument with my daughters and realising how trivial it suddenly seems.

"What would I do without you?" I ask getting up to wash the cups. It's a question that is often posed by the women in our road. Elizabeth has been asked by one of her daughters to move to Scotland to live with her, and we friends and neighbours will miss her if she decides to go.

She is a wise, capable and inspirational woman; our rock.

Elizabeth will be 100 years old next month and, in her own words, "still counting."

130

Memories

By Trisha Todd

"Do you remember the day we met?" He placed his hand over her thin, pale one and looked lovingly at his wife's frail body lying on the metal-framed bed. Eyes closed, her face betrayed little of the stress of recent years, skin smooth but almost translucent now. Grey, wavy hair spread across the starched pillow.

"It was in that little cafe, you know, the one with the piano in the corner – never did see anyone play it. I took one look at you and thought, *Cor, look at those legs.*" He glanced along the bed; the legs he had so admired all those years ago stayed motionless under the pale blue blanket.

"Never thought a beautiful girl like you would look twice at a man like me, being that much older, I mean. It was a bit of luck, meeting you at the dance that evening; must have been fate. I was the only one with a car then – different days, eh? – and you let me drive you home. Made me drop you off at the top of the road though." He smiled at the memory. "Still, must have done something right, we married within the year, and it's not many couples who reach their ruby anniversary nowadays, with the love of their life by their side." A sigh escaped his lips as he shook his head. "Ah, we had some good times, and a few sad ones too, mind you. Our boy

131

moving to New Zealand – oh that was an awful wrench, wasn't it, but we got through it and he's happy. That's life, eh?"

He lapsed into silence for a moment, the stark room they occupied fading from his sight as the memories swirled in his mind.

"Never had a lot of money either, did we love? Didn't make any difference though – if you're happy, you're happy. 'Don't need anything else as long as we have each other' – that's what we used to say. Yes, we had a good life, well, till I had to go away. I didn't want to and it couldn't be helped, but I was sorry about leaving you alone and upsetting you all that time, my darling. Still, I'm here now."

He paused, glancing around the room. His eyes travelled the pale green walls, chipped in places, and the scuffed, grey lino floor, at the television that she never watched, suspended over the bed. They continued on to the electrical panel in the wall, set with lights and buzzer and tubes, and finally to the machinery next to the bed, its steady beep now a sudden continuous tone echoing off the walls.

He took a last look at her prone body, moving to the end of the bed as the door opened and two blue-uniformed nurses rushed in to the room.

"Yes, I promised I'd be here for you now, my darling."

"And we've got eternity together now, my angel," his wife replied with a smile, as their spirits joined.

132

French Getaway

By Barbara Sleap

As I sit here on this high terrace overlooking the lush valley and fields below, memories come flooding back. We have been coming to this hidden hamlet now for 23 years and never seem to tire of our stone cottage surrounded by fields, trees and the gentle hills of the 'Alpes Mancelles' in Normandy. We have been here with our family, we have been here with friends and their families and now we come with our cool, streetwise grandchildren, who surprisingly love the space and freedom that surrounds us.

During our first years here we had no television, no computers, just a crackly radio and a cassette player. Hard to imagine I know, but the children rode bikes, went for country walks and in the evenings we would play silly games. We would have BBQs, drink wine and stay outside until late, watching for shooting stars in the clear night sky, or maybe play boules along the uneven track behind the house until we were no longer able to see the jack.

I can see the wooden gates so lovingly and proudly crafted by my dad, who relished his times here with my mum. Sadly, they are no longer around but we still remember giggling over the photos in their first passports, and the hilarity of my mum's rather pathetic attempt at riding a bike. The puzzlement on their faces whilst trying to decipher a French menu hoping to avoid tripe, tongue or trotters will remain with me. I am truly grateful that we were able to give them so much pleasure. They are not forgotten.

Inside the cottage, the walls are stone and the floor is laid with ancient terracotta tiles, a huge fireplace is the focal point and on our rare winter trips we have a blazing fire which my husband is forever stoking. There are three disconnected bedrooms and a separate washroom across a small courtyard. These bedrooms once accommodated 14 people and resembled temporary dormitories, with much giggling and revelry before sleeping. In the morning, aside from queuing for a shower, there was loud clamouring for the ride to the Boulangerie for fresh bread and the scrumptious croissants that can only be found in France.

Whilst there we visit local markets where you can buy homemade cheese and crème fraiche, home-grown fruit and vegetables, all from local producers and whilst browsing, what better than to enjoy a freshly cooked crepe au chocolat? We have picnics by the river, at the lake or in the grounds of a chateau. Pate, cheese and bread are all that is needed plus, of course, some wine to wash it down. What a feast!

Some things have changed since we purchased our little piece of France. We now have satellite television and a proper oven, and we replaced the steep wooden staircase with a spiral one which looks pretty, but causes you to duck half way down. My husband has treated himself to a small tractor, on which he will happily mow any untended patch of grass in the neighbourhood. In France, he becomes plumber, electrician, mechanic and, unlike at home, he gladly visits any supermarket or street market without a murmur.

The French may have replaced the Franc with the Euro, but the roads are still empty, the villages adorned with flowers in summer and a decent bottle of wine can still be bought for less than three Euros. Snails and tripe remain on the menus, and shops and offices still close for two hours from midday - even the croissants are still the best.

We continue to have wonderful BBQs, play boules along the track, drink wine and play silly games at every opportunity.

So despite our sleepless nights and misgivings those 23 years ago, we can heartily say 'Vive La France'.

136

Singing for his Son

By Debbie Softly

He stood in the wings
His feet felt like lead,
The songs that he wrote
Were fine, sung in bed.

He thought of the nights
The tunes he had hummed,
No one must wake
While guitar he did strum.

The curtains drew back
As he walked on the stage,
He felt like a bird
Released from its cage.

The lyrics were tender
They poured from his heart,
He captured the crowd
Right from the start.

They offered him praise
And waited in line,
They jostled and pushed
With programmes to sign.

He talked to them gently
He talked to each one,
But they weren't aware
He sang for his son.

Staggered

By Sandra Casey

It was 29 October, 2004. It was my birthday the next day. I went to work wondering how had I got to the ripe old age of 33 and accepted it was okay to work on my birthday and to celebrate, probably with a meal out and maybe some drinks on a Friday night.

I normally went straight to my room to set up for teaching, but a few other instructors were in early and they were standing by the reception door. Intriguing? So I diverted to go through the double doors to see what was going on. They were huddled next to a big rucksack and chattering and laughing. As I came through the door they looked startled and then all raised their voices, "Yay, birthday girl!!"

Andy stood there in the background smiling at me. "C'mon old girl we're off!"

It was a daze.

All the kissing and hugging and turning me round to put the backpack on.

The walk from Bank, west towards Euston, berating Andy to tell me what was going on?

"How did he book a day off for me? What's in the backpack? Where are we going?"

He just said, "Trust me, enjoy this."

And so I did.

We parked the bags and shopped a little, drank coffee, chatted, marvelled at buildings (architecture geeks), and lay on the grass to listen to the London buzz all around us and then, towards the evening, had a meal.

I looked across at him and said "I loved today; it's been beautiful... but you know, my birthday is tomorrow."

Laughing out loud, he said "I know that stupid, this is just the beginning. What do you think your bag is for?"

I had been carrying it on and off for most of the day and felt my mouth drop open. Looking at his phone he said it was time to go and he held my hand steering me across traffic lights and crossings to be, suddenly, in front of Euston Station, running for a train! And no ordinary train; it was the sleeper to Fort William!

I have hundreds of joyful memories: giggling trying to get into the bunk, drinking champagne from plastic cups, and the man who got off on his own at a platform in the middle of nowhere and trekked off into the distance. My favourite without question was waking up early at dawn, with the beautiful grey and orange light, thick rolling mist, wide open green and grey landscape. Watched by the soldiers of the mountain, proud stags standing tall on the peaks.

I felt reborn and free.

And loved.

WoSWI

By Barbara Sleap

Reading the paper, a feature caught my eye
Westcliff had started a new WI
I phoned my friend, no need to book
So we thought we'd go and take a look.

The Cliffs was the venue, which we thought select
But we still didn't know quite what to expect.
At the door women queued, it was a good sign
And for one pound fifty we were offered wine.

With some trepidation at a table we sat
And with women of all ages we started to chat
We sang 'Jerusalem' out loud with one voice
So we realised then that we'd made a good choice.

Our meetings are varied, our speakers tell tales
Swishes and raffles, demos and sales.
We hold quizzes, try crafts, sometimes play games
To raise money for charity, these are our aims.

Our subgroups are many, just take your pick
Book groups, or writing, whatever makes you tick
Knitting or choir, cycling or art
Just sign up, it's easy, then you take part.

So now we look forward to twelve Thursdays a year
An evening of company and atmosphere
The committee work hard, not just once a month
So cheers to WoSWI, the best of the bunch.

About the Authors

WoSWI Writing Group

Barbara Sleap

I may be the oldest member of the group, but at 66 I am active and young at heart. I retired from my job as a travel consultant when I was 60 and, so far, I am thoroughly enjoying my retirement. I never seem to get bored, especially as I have five grandchildren to keep me busy.

I became a member of WoSWI two years ago to meet like-minded ladies and to enjoy an interesting night out once a month. I joined one of the book groups and we read a wide range of books and discuss them over tea, and our leader Sue's delicious cakes.

Having always been a scribbler, I was eager to join Kim's writing group which, for me, has been an enlightening and interesting experience. With Kim's guidance I feel my writing now has focus and I love listening to the different styles, and thoughts of my fellow members. I look forward to many more challenges.

My main hobbies apart from books and writing, are travelling whenever possible, keeping fit at my local gym and, as we have a small property in France, I like to relax and enjoy 'La vie Francaise' with family and friends.

Debbie Softly

I was born in Cambridge but moved to Westcliff with my parents when I was six months old. I have remained here ever since so I guess that makes me an Essex Girl! I live with my partner and his 14-year-old disabled son. My two grown-up children still have their base with us, but my daughter mostly works abroad, and my son is at Lincoln University.

In my early 20s I discovered I had a knack for writing rhymes and could usually conjure something up for any occasion or on any subject. I contented myself with this for some years, just doing it for fun, but in my late 30s I tried my hand at a few short stories and articles and I was lucky enough to have a small article published in *Woman's Own*. Sadly work pressure and family commitments lead me to put the writing on the back burner for a while.

Since joining the WoSWI writing group I have now started putting pen to paper or, should I say, fingers to keys once again. It's a great group with everyone encouraging and supporting each other, and in time I plan to start submitting my work in the hope of publication once again.

Josephine Gibson

Josephine, the fourth of five children, was born in County Durham to a family dominated by animals and the country. Her family moved to rural Surrey and then to the wilds of Dartmoor where Josephine grew up.

After leaving home she has lived in London, the Midlands, Surrey and recently, Southend-on-Sea. Her experiences of the solitude of vast open spaces and the chaotic joy of human interaction are reflected in the stories in this anthology.

Karen Richardson

Take one middle aged woman, preferably locally sourced.

Add a loving 1970s' childhood supported by caring parents.

Season with a younger brother.

Stir through a pinch of standard teenage experiences and a large spoonful of secondary education from the 1980s.

Combine the mixture with a marriage in the early 1990s and a precious daughter.

Allow to stand, whilst an amicable divorce, and a period of being a lone parent fortify the final mixture.

If possible, flavour with a very small quantity of employers providing almost 30 years of work.

Fold in strengths and talents which she does not always acknowledge, but knows that others appreciate.

It is worth noting that the finished product is prone to worry, be impatient with herself and to be occasionally self-deprecating, but is dependable and has a lively sense of humour.

Kim Kimber

Kim is a freelance editor and writer. Her work has featured in many publications including *Collect It!*, *Essex Life, Family Camping, Tots to Teens, Wildlife and Countryside, Let's Talk, GY People* and *Writers' News*. Kim is the former Editor of Essex parenting magazine *Step Ahead!*

Studying for a degree in English and History, many moons ago, sparked an interest in local history and in 2010 Kim published *The Southend-on-Sea Quiz Book* as a fun way for local people to learn more about the town they live in. Several more quiz books – this time about musical artists – followed.

Kim joined Westcliff-on-Sea WI (WoSWI) in 2011 to make new friends when her children reached an age where she was no longer needed at the school gates and she missed chatting to other mums. WoSWI had many thriving subgroups but no writing group and so the idea was born.

Having lived in London for most of her adult life, Kim returned to her roots ten years' ago, and now lives by the Thames Estuary which she can just about see through her bedroom window. Putting together this book, like all of Kim's endeavours, has been made easier by the continuing love and support of her husband and three wonderful children.

Lois Maulkin

By day, an assistant shop manager and school kitchen volunteer, by night, an avid reader who dabbles in writing, painting, and singing, and still has no idea what she wants to be when she grows up.

Lois lives in Westcliff-on-Sea, in a small, damp house which she loves. She has four children and a cat that smells.

Lynda Brown

I grew up in the Midlands, moved to London during the '80s and finally settled in Southend with my husband during the '90s. We have two children, and five years ago swapped our roles with me returning to full-time employment as a software test analyst in London, and my husband becoming primary carer for the children at home.

Writing has always been 'something that I would get round to in the future'. The WoSWI writing group has kick-started me and, always one for the dramatic, I find that I prefer to write plays or monologues. I would love to write a drama for television based on my own experiences and using my vivid imagination.

Sandra Casey

I am a dreamer. I navigate by the stars in my Viking ship. I am running in the small cobbled streets of Venice, laughter all around me, face covered by my mask.

I stand on top of a mountain and breathe deeply; the cool air gently caresses my lungs. I swing from the trees and feel my stomach turn somersaults and a wave of joy runs over my body.

I swim with dolphins, fighting to be at the front, weaving in between the boat and my sisters. I feel the sand rough, between my toes. I jump from the bridge, legs tied and bounce back, just as my fingers touch the surface of the water. I ride my stallion, holding tightly to his mane.

I love with all my heart.

I live life. I am a writer.

Trisha Todd

Born in Prittlewell, the fourth of five children, I could read fluently at a very young age and the urge to write stories soon followed. Unfortunately, comments from an over-critical junior school teacher meant I didn't write again until I went to secondary school, where English was my favourite subject.

Story-writing was put aside when I started work as a secretary and, not long after, I met my future husband. We've been married for over 30 years, have three wonderful children and now two beautiful granddaughters.

My eldest daughter and I joined Westcliff-on-Sea Women's Institute where, a short time later, a writing group was formed. I joined up straight away and have made some new friends at the fun monthly meetings. I didn't really know what I wanted to accomplish beyond finding out if I could still write. However, after entering a poetry competition in *Writing Magazine* a short time later, I was pleasantly surprised to discover it had come second, and now I never leave the house without my notepad and pencil.

I hope that you will enjoy reading my attempts.

Westcliff-on-Sea Women's Institute

WESTCLIFF-ON-SEA
WOMEN'S INSTITUTE

(Registered Charity No. XT 36711)

From hoteliers to decorators, teachers to full-time mums, there isn't a typical member of Westcliff-on-Sea Women's Institute (affectionately known as WoSWI). We come from all walks of life and cover all age ranges.

Based in Westcliff-on-Sea in Essex, what we do have in common is a dedication to having fun, enjoying the company of interesting women, broadening our horizons and occasionally indulging in the odd tipple.

Each year we vote on a local charity to support, based on members' suggestions. This year we're supporting Southend Hospital Brachytherapy Appeal and hope to match the fundraising success of past years.

Our interests cover crafts, culture, education and social activities. Since our first meeting in September 2009, hundreds of women have come along to see what WoSWI is all about.

www.westcliffwi.co.uk

The Brachytherapy Suite Appeal

Southend Hospital
CHARITY

(Registered Charity No. 1057266)

The Brachytherapy Appeal aims to raise £140,000 to buy equipment for Southend Hospital's new brachytherapy suite, due to open in late summer 2013.

Brachytherapy is a new high-tech and intense way of treating cancer. High dose brachytherapy (HDR) uses a miniature, highly active, radiation source to precisely target the affected area of people suffering with certain cancers such as skin, gynaecological, breast, oesophageal, and medium-risk prostate cancer.

Brachytherapy offers enormous benefits to patients, enabling them to be treated as outpatients, rather than stay in hospital and shorter treatment times.

Southend University Hospital is one of only about 10 centres in the UK, and the only one in Essex, to offer this high-tech treatment.

The new suite will have its own theatre and treatment lounge but money is urgently needed to buy equipment including an operating table.

3700770R00091

Printed in Great Britain
by Amazon.co.uk, Ltd.,
Marston Gate.